HONKY

&

THE GREAT BIG PIG HEIST

ORLA
KELLY
PUBLISHING

MARGARET M. GRIFFIN

Illustrated by Helen Joy

This book would not have been written without Honky,
so it is dedicated to her and to all pigs everywhere.
Also, I'd like to dedicate this story to all the children who will, one day,
need to make hard decisions to protect our world and the animals.

Contents

1.

Annie

Annie yawned and rubbed the sleep from her eyes as the baby bottles whirred around and around the microwave. She longed to be tucked up in her warm bed instead of heating milk in her cold kitchen in the dead of night. She was beginning to realise looking after twelve babies was hard work, much harder than she expected.

Outside, Annie couldn't even see the first faint fingers of light in the morning sky. The whole world was still asleep, and only the gentle purr of the microwave could be heard in the early morning quiet.

But she knew that peace wouldn't last for long. She watched the digital clock on the microwave as it counted down, 5...4...3...2...1. The microwave suddenly gave a loud '*PING*', and that's when all hell broke loose.

'Sqweeeeee!' came the cry of the first piglet, and his excited squeal was quickly following by a chorus of the others.

'Sqweeeeee! Sqweeeeee! Sqweeeeee! Sqweeeeee!'

The cottage was suddenly filled with the sound of high-pitched and ear-piercing squeals. If Annie spoke pig language, she would have understood the clamour of tiny voices coming from the box in her porch.

'Weeeeeeeee! It's food time!'

'Me, first!'

'No, me!'

'Get off! You're standing on me!'

'Yay! Milk time, my favourite!'

'I'm soooo hungry. Oooh, I'm soooo hungry!'

'Weeeeeeeee! Food time!'

But all Annie heard was the rumpus of hungry piglets demanding their milk.

'I'm coming... I'm coming,' she sighed as she gathered up the half a dozen baby bottles filled with warm milk.

Annie thought about their mother, no doubt still happily snoring in her shed. She wondered why she rejected her piglets and refused to nurse them. It all started so well. Annie had watched from a distance as Lady Lavinia, fondly known as Lady L, began to make a nest for her piglets. She dragged long wet grass, rushes and ferns and wove them around a damp, flattened mud hollow. She started to give birth to her piglets in this nest the very next day.

But something must have disturbed her because Lady L left the nest and started giving birth to other piglets in various locations around the field. As soon as Annie saw the scattered piglets, she knew there was something wrong. She could see by Lady L's pacing and angry snorting that she was distressed.

'What's the matter, Lady L?' Annie asked. 'Are you in pain? Did something upset you?'

She tried to reach out and stroke her, but Lady L snorted in irritation and fled the comforting hand.

Annie saw her snapping at the piglets they tried to suckle from her, and she gasped in horror when she spotted one of the piglet's tails hanging off by a thread of skin. Lady L must have stood on the poor piglet! Annie knew she couldn't delay any longer. Lady Lavinia's normal mothering instincts weren't kicking in. She was behaving aggressively towards the piglets, and they were in danger.

She rushed back to the house, found a big box and stuffed it with straw. Then she ran back to the field and, in the driving rain, gathered up all twelve wriggling piglets and placed them in the cosy box. Back at the cottage, she rummaged in the kitchen until she found her old feeding bottles and filled them with milk.

Lady L will be back to herself by tomorrow, and I'll put back her piglets, and everything will be fine again, she thought. Annie was convinced that once the sow settled down, she would reunite her with her piglets.

Meanwhile, Annie knew she faced a round-the-clock job because piglets feed little and often from the sow and sleep in a warm heap on top of each other afterwards. The baby bottles were difficult to introduce to the piglets, but one by one, as the milk trickled out and ran down their snouts, they knew what to do. They realised that if they suckled hard enough, they got loads more warm, creamy milk.

Once the piglets' tummies were full, they became sleepy, and peace resumed as they snuggled down to snooze. But within an hour, Annie needed to prepare more bottles, and the uproar would begin again.

Annie continued to feed the piglets all day and even got up several times during that night. The next afternoon, after Lady L had time to recover from the labour, Annie tried to reintroduce the piglets.

'Look, Lady L, I have all your beautiful babies here,' said Annie, lifting the lovely piglets out of the box and placing them in her enclosure. But Lady Lavinia turned up her snout and showed complete disinterest. She didn't even sniff them and only snorted and stamped her hoof as the tiny piglets milled around her. Fearing that the sow might trample or crush the piglets, Annie brought them home again. That's when Annie realised she had become the piglets' full-time surrogate mother.

The piglets got very noisy, very fast. They squealed at the tops of their voices because they learnt very early that their loud cries brought milk. Annie often crept down the stairs early in the morning so the piglets wouldn't hear her. But once they heard that 'ping' of the microwave, their eyes sprang open, they scrambled to their feet, and they squealed with all their might.

One morning, Annie arrived into the front porch, warm bottles under her arms. The excitement reached fever pitch.

'Sqweeeeee! Sqweeeeee! Sqweeeeee! Sqweeeeee!' the piglets went, their high-pitched squeals filling the cottage. The larger piglets were standing on their hind hooves scrambling against the box, desperate to be the first to be lifted out and fed.

Annie fed them in rotation, knowing each of the piglets by their distinctive markings. After each feed, she let the piglet down to exercise around the box and pee or poo on newspapers laid on the floor. She was surprised at how clean they were and how they always chose the same spot. It made cleaning up after the piglets easy.

As she reached in to feed the largest and most demanding piglet, she caught a glimpse of a piglet curled up in the far corner of the box. She was motionless and quite unlike all her siblings jumping up and down as they squealed for their milk.

Annie's heart sank as she reached in to scoop the sleeping pig from the melee.

'Oh, poor sick little piggy!' she said. 'Whatever is the matter?'

'Forget about her, what about meeeeee?' cried one piglet.

'Put her down, I'm hungreeeee!' squealed another.

But Annie only had eyes for the Sick Little Piggy lying silent and lifeless in her arms.

2.

Sick Little Piggy

Sick Little Piggy had only a vague memory of Annie gently washing her, cleaning off the diarrhoea and tiny hoof prints on her skin, and placing her in a small polystyrene box filled with clean straw. She stirred as Annie tucked a hot water bottle with a soft, fleecy turquoise cover under her. She would have stretched in bliss, but she was much too tired. Her new home was nice and quiet, and none of her siblings could trample on her anymore. She liked this feeling of being warm and clean.

She even managed to open one eye to watch Annie move about the kitchen. She saw her boil the kettle and let it cool before adding a teaspoon of salt and sugar to the water. Then she saw her fiddle with a small plastic syringe. Suddenly, Annie was looming over her and trying to force the watery mixture into her snout. Sick Little Piggy didn't feel like eating, and she didn't like this liquid at all. She squealed very loudly in protest, but Annie persisted.

'I promise this will make you feel better,' she said.

'That's disgusting!' Honky replied, but all Annie heard was a weak oink.

Fighting off the syringe was all too much for Sick Little Piggy, and she fell into a deep, deep sleep.

Much later, she opened an eye again and saw Annie and a strange woman peering down at her.

'Yes, she's got scour all right,' the woman said, squinting in at the piglet from behind her spectacles. 'Scour is an infection that causes diarrhoea. Many newborn animals can get this, particularly when they haven't had their mother's first milk called colostrum. The diarrhoea makes them so dehydrated that they can die.'

She handled and prodded Sick Little Piggy gently and nodded her head.

'You did the right thing, Annie,' she said. 'You got to her just in time and saved her life with sugar and saltwater. Keep it up, tiny amounts very often, and start her on this course of antibiotics, and this little piggy should be feeling better very soon!'

After the woman left, Sick Little Piggy saw that Annie was smiling broadly.

'See? The vet said you will be just fine,' she said as she stroked her. 'You're going to get all better.'

'I just want to nap now,' grunted Sick Little Piggy.

But she did feel better when she woke again that night. And when Annie came to her with a bottle of milk, she yawned and stretched lazily.

'Yes, I feel a little peckish,' she decided. She sucked on the bottle for a whole half a minute before tiredness overcame her again. She didn't see Annie beaming with joy as she watched her quietly snore.

The next day, Sick Little Piggy didn't feel so sick anymore. Nor did she feel so tired. She attempted to scramble to her feet, but nothing happened.

'Come on legs, move!' she said, but not a single trotter moved.

What's going on? My legs are not working anymore, thought Sick Little Piggy. So, she tried again and again until she felt breathless from the exertion, and yet her feet didn't move.

When Annie came to feed her, she realised that Sick Little Piggy was struggling to get on her feet.

'Poor Sick Little Piggy,' she said. 'You're still a bit weak, but we'll feed you up, and you'll be as right as rain again.'

Sick Little Piggy liked the sound of being cured by feeding.

But this time, Annie wasn't right. She fed Sick Little Piggy lots of rich, creamy warm milk, but the piglet still couldn't get back on her feet the next day or the day after that. Her legs felt like jelly and no longer obeyed her. She had to wriggle around on her belly or her side to move anywhere.

'What's going on?' she squealed, but Annie looked worried and didn't tell her she'd soon be better anymore.

Sick Little Piggy woke up to find Annie and the vet peering down at her again one day.

'She seems paralysed,' Annie said. 'She's not able to stand anymore and is just about able to drag herself around.'

The vet handled Sick Little Piggy and pulled at her legs and tail and felt down the length of her back, and then she scratched her head.

'I don't know what's going on,' she said. 'Everything appears fine, and the fact that she's drinking milk is a very good sign.'

'I had hoped to put her back in with the other piglets by now,' said Annie. 'But they're too boisterous and rough for her while she's in this condition.'

'No, you need to keep her separate from the others,' agreed the vet.

'Do you think she's going to be okay?' asked Annie, her expression worried.

Sick Little Piggy saw the vet shrug her shoulders.

'All I can say is keep doing what you're doing,' she said. 'Where there's life, there's hope.'

Sick Little Piggy didn't want to be left alone lying in her box. She wanted to be back with her piggy brothers and sisters.

'Put me back with everyone else!' she cried. 'Please, put me back!'

But the vet and Annie only heard her sad little oinks.

3.

Honky

Annie couldn't understand why Sick Little Piggy was paralysed. The day that she brought the piglets into her house, she had recorded them all on video. She watched and re-watched the video, and she could see that Sick Little Piggy was just as strong and active as her siblings.

Sick Little Piggy had a white face, but most of her hair was red, and she had distinctive black spots on her back. She was easy to spot among the litter in the video.

She watched Sick Little Piggy wriggle in her box as she tried to get on her feet.

'Could you have had a stroke from dehydration?' she wondered aloud.

'I don't know,' Sick Little Piggy replied. 'All I know are my legs won't work anymore.'

But again, Annie only heard oinks and grunts.

'If it's a stroke, I guess we have to give the same treatment that's given to any stroke patient,' she decided.

So, Annie devised a programme designed to exercise Sick Little Piggy's leg muscles. She even suspended the piglet from a small sheet to help put weight on her back legs. Sick Little Piggy screamed the place down during that exercise.

'Ouch! Ouch!' she squealed. 'Put me down! Put me down this minute! I don't like this at all!'

Annie also placed Sick Little Piggy in the garden every morning after her breakfast even though she could barely lift her head. As a result, Sick Little Piggy found her snout stuck in the grass and the mud, and she screamed in protest.

'Lift me out of here!' she cried. 'Take me back to my nice warm box!'

'Every little piggy needs to get iron from mud,' Annie tried to explain. 'It's good for you. It should be instinct to dig your snout into the ground to get that iron.'

Sick Little Piggy soon stopped complaining. She realised she liked the taste of the mud and the feeling of soft grass underneath her. She grunted happily in the garden and liked to watch Annie working nearby.

Annie was a smallholder - a very small farmer - who loved animals. Even as a young girl growing up in Dublin city, she was used to finding sick animals and caring for them. She once found a baby magpie that had fallen out of a nest, and she put him in a box and nursed him back to health. Her mother blamed her years afterwards for the huge magpie population of that part of Dublin.

One night, her dad let the dog out to have a wee, and the dog spotted a kitten in the garden and chased her down. Annie ran out screaming and rescued the poor mite.

When she moved down the country, she kept ducks and chickens and even horses and ponies when her children were small. She always had an assortment of dogs and cats as pets. She discovered a neighbouring farmer trying to force the faces of two kittens into saucers of milk one day. Their mother had been killed, and the old bachelor farmer was trying to feed them. But they were much too tiny to lap, and he had almost drowned them in milk instead. She managed to save those kittens too, even taking them on the family camping holiday in the West of Ireland so that she could bottle feed them around the clock.

Annie became friends with a farmer who lived on a big dairy farm nearby. The woman fattened a couple of pigs for her family in a walled garden on the farm. Annie saw this woman feeding the pigs barley and milk straight from the cows. She watched the pigs rooting about under apple trees, in long grass and among sweet flowers in the old walled garden. Annie loved sitting and watching them and became fascinated by pigs.

This is how pigs should be reared - not in concrete sheds, she thought. Every time she left the dairy farm, she said to herself, I must get pigs. She said this for years. Then one day, she decided to do it and bought two pigs, Lady Lavinia and the boar, Laertes. She never looked back.

Together, Lady Lavinia and Laertes had had lots of piglets, and Annie sold most of them to people wanting to rear free-range pigs for themselves. She also kept a few for herself and her customers. Some piglets lived on her small farm for ten months before a short trip to the small abattoir down in the village.

Sick Little Piggy was just another in a long line of animals that Annie had rescued and rehabilitated. But no matter what she did, this patient wasn't improving. She was stumped. She was very fond of Sick Little Piggy and was afraid of what the vet might say if she didn't get better soon.

Annie and her son Ben were in the garden one day watching Sick Little Piggy wriggling in the grass.

'I've tried lots of exercises, and I've tried leaving her here to move around by herself, but she's not getting better,' she sighed.

'She loves her food, though, doesn't she?' said Ben.

'She's got a great appetite alright.'

'Let me try something then when it's time for her next feed.'

When it was time for Sick Little Piggy's next bottle, Ben held it enticingly just out of the piglet's reach, so she had to stretch and move to get it.

Sick Little Piggy was outraged and squealed in protest.

'This is torture!' she cried. 'This boy should be reported to the pig police for cruelty!'

Sick Little Piggy couldn't help herself, though. She wriggled, and she squirmed, and she crawled after that bottle. Every evening, Ben carried Sick Little Piggy into the garden and tortured her with the moving bottle and forced her to exercise. Sick Little Piggy got faster and stronger, wriggling after her bottle.

One day when Ben moved the bottle out of reach again, the piglet suddenly scrambled to her feet and staggered towards it.

'Mum! Mum, come quick!' Ben yelled with excitement.

Annie rushed into the garden and clapped her hands over her mouth in shock at the sight.

'Look, she's on her feet!' cried a triumphant Ben.

'It's a miracle!' laughed Annie.

'It's torture!' cried Sick Little Piggy. 'Just give me my bottle!'

The next day Annie put the bottle in the microwave, and as soon as Sick Little Piggy heard the 'ping,' she staggered towards the kitchen honking loudly.

'Give me my bottle! Give me my bottle!' cried Sick Little Piggy.

But Annie was too busy crying.

'Look at you - oh, my goodness, look at you on all four feet!' she sobbed. 'And what a racket you're making. *Honk, honk, honk.* I think I'll have to call you Honky!'

From then on, Sick Little Piggy became known as Honky.

4.

Lonely

Honky was excited when Annie told her that she didn't have long to wait before reuniting with all her brothers and sisters.

'I think you're almost ready,' she said. 'Another day or two, you'll be a little bit stronger and steadier on your feet.'

Honky often heard the other piglets playing in the vegetable patch when she was in the garden. She could also listen to them from her box in Annie's front porch, but she hadn't seen her siblings in many weeks. So she squealed with excitement the day that Annie picked her up to put her into their pen.

'I'm back!' she cried. 'It's me. I'm back!'

But Honky's siblings didn't pay any attention. Instead, they swarmed around Annie, who sat on the stool she used every time she bottle-fed them. But one by one, as the piglets were fed, they noticed Honky among them. Honky's biggest sister, Stumpy, eyed her first. She was called Stumpy after her tail had to be removed because her mother stood on it shortly after birth. Then Honky's biggest brother, Red Lad, who was red with a white stripe around his middle like a Saddleback pig, stared too. They both approached and started to nudge and then shove her.

'What are you doing here? We don't want you. You don't belong here anymore,' they said.

Annie watched for a few minutes and didn't intervene, but they knocked Honky about, hitting her harder and harder until she squealed.

'Why are you hitting me? Why don't you want me here? Annie, get me out of here!' she cried.

Then the rest of the litter surrounded her and, following the lead of Stumpy and Red Lad, started head-butting and biting her. That's when Annie lifted her out.

'Oh, poor little Honky,' she said. 'Don't worry. They'll grow to love you like I do. We'll try again tomorrow.'

Annie tried to reintroduce Honky to the litter the next day and the days following. She even left her with them for a while. But Honky was miserable. The others picked on her, bullied her unmercifully and knocked her over.

'Out! Out! You don't belong here anymore,' they told her.

In the end, Annie had to admit defeat.

'I think they would have accepted her eventually,' Honky heard her tell the vet. 'But they would always have bullied her. I was afraid that she would never recover properly.'

Honky was sad because she knew his brothers and sisters didn't want her. She realised she was going to have to make her home with Annie and the dogs. Annie was lovely, but the dogs were jealous. They didn't like how Annie allowed her in the house and how she petted and scratched her.

'We're Annie's favourites, not you. Stay away!' they growled.

Honky was getting too big for the front porch. So, when Annie moved all the piglets to their new grown-up house, she moved Honky into the woodshed in the vegetable patch on her own. She wanted to make Honky feel at home, so she took the dog bed that Honky used in the house and placed it under the oil tank in the shed. She also filled the area with golden straw.

But Annie still worried about Honky the first night the piglet slept outside. She was afraid that Honky might be cold, frightened or lonely. So, that evening, she went out to her hut to check on her. She was alarmed to find the dog bed empty and no sign of her little red piglet.

'Honky? Honky? Where are you?' she called, panicked.

Suddenly, the dog bed appeared to levitate in the air, and Honky's sleepy snout, studded with stalks of straw, appeared underneath it. Honky hadn't been able to decide which she liked best - her bed or the straw. So, she sandwiched herself between them both and had fallen fast asleep. Annie laughed and laughed at the sight of Honky wearing her big dog bed hat.

Annie always left Honky's gate open during the day, so the little red piglet had a lot more freedom than the other piglets. The farmer only locked up Honky safely in her pen in the vegetable patch at night. So, Honky was able to come and go and ramble around the farm all day, and she soon got into a bit of a routine.

Every morning, Honky woke to the sound of the dogs barking with excitement as Annie let them out. The barking was the cue for Honky to immediately start pacing up and down and honking and squealing loudly for Annie.

'Annnnnnie, let me out! Let me out!' she'd cry. She'd squeal even louder with delight as she saw her coming up the field.

Honky followed Annie around the farm every morning. The hens and ducks had to be let out and fed first thing. Honky waited until Annie's back was turned before she sneaked into the hens and ducks' pen to rob some of their feed.

'Honky, you little devil!' Annie would shout. 'Shoo! Out, out, shoooo!'

Honky thought it was great fun. She followed Annie as she fed her siblings and her parents, Lady L and Laertes. At every point along the way, Honky managed to get her snout in some extra feed. She loved the morning routine with Annie.

Afterwards, she mooched about the garden and sometimes, she popped into the house for a snooze on the dogs' beds. Annie always laughed when she found her in the dogs' beds, and she scratched and tickled her. But the dogs were not happy, and they glowered and growled.

'Go away, Honky!' they said. 'A pig is not meant to be in the house. Go and stay with the other pigs. The house is for us, not you!'

But Honky was getting bigger and braver, and she didn't let them push her around.

'Annie says I can go in the house, and it's her house!' she retorted.

When Annie wasn't around, however, Honky felt lonely. Some days, Annie went to work in a job far away from the farm. The dogs and the fat cat were about the place, but they didn't want anything to do with Honky. All three spent a lot of the time growling at her. The fat cat liked to sleep in the sun on top of Annie's herbs and got very annoyed when Honky rooted him out of the way with her snout. Even the pigs told her to go away when she stuck her nose in their pen for a chat.

Often, when there was no one to talk to or no one to play with, Honky was a very lonely piglet indeed.

5.

The Boy

One day, it was even quieter than usual. Annie had gone to work, and the dogs had been left in the house because she didn't trust them around the new ducklings. The pigs never talked to her. The ducks were busy with their ducklings, and the hens were rooting and scratching together under the hedges. Honky even went to check on the cat, but he was asleep as usual. Honky felt very sad and lonely, and she sighed and wandered to the front gate. Maybe she could see some exciting things on the road, or she might spot Annie's car returning.

Instead, the most extraordinary thing happened: a small boy appeared on the far side of the gate out of nowhere. Honky leapt back with fright and stared at the boy. He had jet black hair, translucent pale skin and piercing blue eyes. He was spotlessly dressed in a neat brown tweed jacket, and even his wellies were shiny. Honky never saw a child on his own on the road before. The people who usually passed were big like Annie. They walked, cycled or drove past at speed to avoid Annie's crazy barking dogs.

The boy approached the gate and pushed his hand in between the bars. Honky came closer to the entrance to sniff the hand. The boy giggled and jumped back. But he shoved his hand through again. This time Honky rubbed her muddy snout into the hand, and the boy shrieked and jumped back again.

The boy didn't make the same sounds as Annie or other people. Instead, Honky thought he was making grunting sounds. The little piglet turned her head to one side and studied the boy.

'I wonder if you are trying to copy me?' Honky grunted aloud, more to herself than anything because humans never understood her.

But the boy shook his head and said, 'This is the way I talk.'

Honky was startled because humans never understood her before.

'You know what I'm saying?' she asked.

'Of course,' said the boy. 'And you can understand me?'

'I understand people,' said Honky. 'They just never understand me.'

'I guess we're the same because people don't understand me either,' said the boy.

Honky was delighted to find someone she could talk to and play with.

'Why don't you open the gate and come in?' she said.

The boy rattled the gate again and again, but Honky saw that he couldn't open it the way Annie always did.

The boy gave up and put his hand in the gate, and this time he didn't jump away when Honky stuck her snout into his palm for a good sniff.

The boy didn't speak much after that, and Honky got distracted by a delicious looking grub that she spotted wriggling under the yew tree. When she came back a few minutes later, he was gone.

6.

Adventures

The next day Honky was back at the big yew tree in the corner of the garden. She liked rooting under it because Annie threw all the grass clippings there, and Honky found loads of grubs and tasty worms under the rotting grass. Honky stopped rooting when she heard loud shouting. The dogs were out, and she saw them charging to the gate, barking loudly.

'Who are you? Get away! This is our house! You're not welcome!' they yelled.

Honky followed them and saw the small boy at the gate again. The boy didn't like the noise the dogs were making, and he backed away, his eyes shut and his hands over his ears. The dogs kept barking until Annie whistled for them, and then they charged back into the house.

'Noisy creatures, aren't they?' said Honky, and the boy took his hands from his ears in relief and nodded in agreement.

He pushed his hand through the gate, and this time neither shouted nor jumped back when Honky nuzzled him with his mucky snout.

Honky saw the boy wrestle with the gate again, but he couldn't open it, and neither could she. So, they stood looking at each other instead.

'I'm Honky. Who are you?' said the piglet, finally remembering her manners.

'I'm Hugo,' said the boy. 'How do you do?'

'I'm well, thank you. But I wish you could come in to play.'

As they couldn't play with the big gate in the way, they chatted, and if anyone had overheard them, they would have only heard an exchange of grunts and mumbles. Hugo told Honky he lived only two houses away down the road, but he didn't know anyone as his family had only moved to the area months ago.

'Why do you sound so different to all the other people?' Honky asked.

Hugo shrugged.

'I just do. I understand everyone, but they don't understand me. My parents don't seem to think I'm different to other children. They say I'll grow out of it.'

Hugo said he used to watch the pigs because he could see them from his bedroom window.

'I was a bit scared of the lady who looks after you all in case she might be cross if I called to see you,' he said.

'That's Annie,' explained Honky. 'She looks after us all on the farm, and she's lovely. She's never cross!'

Hugo explained that, finally, he couldn't resist the temptation anymore, so he slipped out of the back of his house, came out through a gap in the hedge and walked a short bit down the road, and that is how he met Honky at the gate for the first time.

Hugo continued to come to the gate at the same time every day, and Honky came to stand on the other side of it. Hugo was persistent, and every day he tried to get in.

'I wish we could play,' said Honky.

'So do I,' sighed Hugo.

But it was impossible to play when there was a big gate separating them.

Then one day, Honky was rooting about under the yew tree near the gate, and a noise startled her. Annie had forced a big pallet into a gap beside a fence post to stop the dogs from getting out onto the road.

Honky spotted Hugo on his knees at this part of the fence. He was trying to squeeze between the pallet and the fence post with rusty barbed wire dangling around both.

'Be careful, Hugo!' cried Honky as she watched the boy trying to squeeze and wriggle his way through. But a strand of barbed wire caught Hugo's clothes, and there was a loud ripping sound. Suddenly Hugo's jacket had a huge hole in it. Hugo wailed as he pulled off his torn coat and held it up to examine it.

'Oh no!' he cried. 'Look what I did!'

Honky was confused.

'Why are you crying? Stuff is nice when it's battered and torn,' she said. But Hugo didn't seem to agree, so Honky snuffled at him and tried to nip him and tickle him until Hugo laughed aloud.

Honky was delighted because she had a playmate at last.

'Let's go exploring!' she said. 'Follow me!'

Honky led Hugo up into the field behind the henhouse towards Farmer Herbert's fields.

'Don't touch that fence because it hurts when you touch it,' she warned. 'But I know a secret way behind it.'

Without Annie's knowledge, Honky had figured out how to get under the fence. There was one part of the fence, right behind the henhouse, where the land sloped and dipped into Farmer Herbert's field. When Honky sat on her haunches, she could slide right under the fence into the other meadow. On the other side, she paddled across a drain with a stream of water, and then she snuffled and snorted her way through a lovely big, grassy green meadow. Farmer Herbert wasn't using his fields because it was still winter, and the outdoors was too wet and muddy for his cows. It was perfect for a pig, though!

Hugo watched as the piglet slid underneath the fence and down into the other field.

'Weeeeee!' Honky squealed in delight.

Honky could see that Hugo didn't like muck or dirt because he made a few 'ugh!' faces. Still, he wriggled his way under the fence feet first and slid down into the next field on his bottom. He shrieked as the cold water in the drain ran into his wellies. Hugo clambered to his feet and looked down at himself. His jacket was torn; he was covered in mud, and his wellies were wet. Then he started giggling and Honky snorted, and they laughed and laughed.

They didn't know it then, but that day was the start of all their adventures.

7.

Hugo

Hugo's shoulders were slumped as he got off the school bus and walked up the drive to his house. Not from the weight of his school bag, which was substantial, but because the burden of the day weighed heavily on his shoulders. He hated school. He hated every minute he was there.

Every day, he felt tense and on edge, a bit like some children feel before a difficult school exam. However, tests end and the pressure lifts, but Hugo's burden stayed with him every day.

Today, as he turned his key in the front door, he felt happier and lighter. He would slip out and meet Honky again today. He was always happier now when he knew he would spend part of his day with Honky. They would go exploring together and have lots of fun. Finally, he had something to look forward to.

He saw his minder in the living room glued to her usual quiz show.

'There's a sandwich in the kitchen for you,' Molly called without even turning around from the TV.

'Thank you,' he replied, even though she never understood what he said.

It was the same dry old cheese sandwich she made every day. It was always waiting for him because she didn't like to be disturbed during her quiz shows. And there seemed to be quiz shows on all day. Molly was usually on the phone or smoking in the back garden if she wasn't watching TV. He sat at the table and took a bite out of his sandwich.

Hugo's parents were older than most other mothers and fathers of children his age. They worked full time in academic jobs in the university, and they hired Molly to look after him.

Hugo started school in the village after they recently moved into the area, but he wasn't fitting in. The teachers and the other children didn't understand him, so they mostly ignored him.

He found school more difficult than most children because he couldn't bear loud noises. During little break and lunch break, when all the children streamed out and played football or chattered in the rain shelter, the sound was almost unbearable to his ears. The noise drove him to run behind the shelter even if it was raining. Often, he came back into the class soaking wet and sat in the room steaming as his clothes dried off. Sometimes this led to a chest infection, so he was off school for at least a week.

Being off school was bliss for Hugo. He could stay at home in an oasis of calm while his parents were away all day. Molly the minder was always watching TV, so she never bothered him. But Hugo was lonely without friends.

He often stared out his bedroom window for hours at a time, and that's how he became fascinated by the pigs in the fields near him. He was so glad that he met Honky at the gate that day because he had found a friend and someone who understood him at last.

Yes, things were looking up for Hugo. He was excited about all the places he and Honky could explore together.

He popped his head in the sitting room door just as the quiz show host was announcing a new contestant.

'I have to go outside for a while for a school project I'm doing,' Hugo said. He had to collect five wildflowers for a nature project the class had been assigned. It wouldn't be easy considering it was mid-winter, but he could ask Honky to help him. Or at least he could ask her not to eat every flower head she saw.

But Molly never lifted her eyes from the television.

'Yeah, whatever', she said.

Hugo hopped over his garden wall into the field beside his family home. He had to pass a small cottage, now being used as an office in the field. Sometimes the people inside saw him, but they just waved. He walked to the corner of the field until he reached the fence to the road. He climbed through a gap and ran a short distance on the road until he saw the pallet into Annie's farm marked near the big yew tree. Once he gave the pallet a rattle, Honky appeared.

'Hi, Hugo! Good to see you!' said a delighted Honky.

'Ha-ha-ha-ha-ha,' is all Annie or anyone else would have heard. Annie, with her experience, would have instantly recognised those breathy grunts as the greeting sound of a pig when they are pleased to see someone. But Hugo didn't need experience with pigs. He understood everything Honky said.

'Honky, I have to collect some samples for nature class at school. Will we go around the fields and explore together again?'

'Great!' grunted Honky. She wiggled her tail and did a happy spin, and Hugo burst out laughing.

'You are funny,' he said.

'I aim to please,' Honky replied but had to sit down for a spell as the spinning made her dizzy.

The two of them darted up Annie's field, slipped around the back of the henhouse and slid down the slope into the drain. After that, they wandered Farmer

Herbert's extensive meadows and the country laneways, and as they went, Hugo collected his flowers – a sweet violet here and a snowdrop there.

They trundled across the fields together, and anyone who spotted them would have thought they looked a strange sight - a tall, dark-haired thin boy accompanied by a small, rotund red pig. But no one saw them. The fields and surrounding laneways were quiet because farmers hadn't begun to let their cattle out yet, so they had little reason to be outside their farmyards. The slide into Farmer Herbert's field was only one way, so they had to return to their respective homes the long way. Hugo always brought Honky back to Annie's place. He made a quick dart along the road where the piglet squeezed in by the pallet before Hugo ran home himself. The boy and the pig were free to wander around all that winter; two friends wrapped up in their own little world.

8.

Falling for a Farmer

Annie yawned as she topped up the teapot with fresh boiling water. She had to be at work early today. She was jolted awake by the sound of her dogs' furious barks shattering the early morning peace.

Annie opened the back door and saw a jeep parked outside the front gates. She could see a figure standing there under the trees, so she grabbed her coat and followed the dogs. Annie kept a lock on the gate to stop anyone from opening it and leaving it open. She was always amazed at the number of people who left farm gates open after visiting, never thinking that the animals inside are intrinsically nosy and will always come out to explore. It was even more dangerous in Annie's case because her farm gate led to a busy road. She was always worried that Honky or the dogs would get out and get hit or cause an accident, so she kept the gates firmly locked.

'Shush, shush! Quieten down!' she called. The dogs were leaping around the gate and yelling at the tops of their voices at the potential intruder.

Farmer Herbert was standing on the other side of the gate looking cross, but he always looked cross. Annie knew it was never good news when her next-door neighbour Alex Herbert called.

'Hiya Alex, what's up?' asked Annie.

'Annie, your pigs are escaping into my field. My son saw them yesterday and the day before.'

'Oh no! They're little brats,' replied Annie, biting her tongue so she didn't mention all the times she found his cattle in her fields.

'I searched yesterday to find where they're getting out,' she said. 'I thought I had fixed the gap, but they must be getting out somewhere else. I promise I'll get down to the stores before they close and get a new battery for the fence.'

Mollified, Farmer Herbert muttered something about a 'grand day' before springing into his jeep and driving off.

After work, Annie raced down the Boarswood Road to the agri stores. She would have preferred to go straight home and enjoy a long, hot bath, but she didn't want another visit from frowning Farmer Herbert. She had to get that battery and install it first thing in the morning before letting the pigs out again. She checked the clock on the dashboard. She should just make it before closing. The rain lashed down as she reached the stores. She pulled her coat hood up over her head and dashed across the car park to the door. Blinded by the oversized hood, she shoved the door forcibly at the exact time someone else was pulling it inside the shop. Annie stumbled inside, lurching straight into the man who opened the door. She clutched at him desperately and managed to steady herself rather than end up on the floor.

'Oh, goodness!' she cried. 'I'm so sorry!'

She looked up at the man into whose arms she had flung herself.

'No harm done,' he said with an amused smile. 'Nasty day out there, isn't it?'

She straightened up and swept back the wet strand of hair that had fallen into her face. Her cheeks were tinged with red from embarrassment.

The man was tall and well-built. He was also familiar looking.

'Yes, well, sorry again,' she said, flustered. 'I really must look where I'm going next time!'

Then Annie turned on her heel and fled down the fertilizer aisle. It took her a minute or two to remember. She had seen him around the village before, and someone said he was a local pig farmer. *James, yes, that's his name,* she thought. But that's all she knew about him.

9.

James

James was still smiling as he crossed the car park, despite the teeming rain. He was thinking about the woman who had thrown herself into his arms. He chuckled as he remembered her embarrassment and how she couldn't wait to escape from him. *She looks familiar,* he thought. I must ask Syl about her next time I'm back in the stores.

But James sighed as he sat into his jeep and turned the key in the ignition. *No rest for the wicked,* he thought as he recalled the endless list of things he had to do at home. James always referred to himself as a reluctant farmer. And these days, he felt even more reluctant. There never seemed to be enough hours in the day to get everything done.

The pig farm didn't earn enough money to keep him, so James had another job in a nearby factory where they recycled plastic. Working shifts as one of the line managers there, he could also juggle the jobs on the farm. James had a couple of part-time helpers who looked after the pigs while he was at work. Apart from that, he never really thought about the animals. After doing something the same way all his life, farming had become automatic.

In the past, when the countryside was filled with small family farms, most farmers kept a couple of pigs in a sty. Often, they were confined for their lives in a tiny pen and fed scraps from the household. Wiser farmers let the pigs out to plough through the vegetable patch. With their digging and rooting, the pigs did all the labour and got the ground ready for planting again. James' father started with a couple of pigs like most farmers. But he decided to make a business of them and increased the herd of pigs on the farm.

By the time his father retired and James took over the farm, there were about 300 pigs. His pig farm was still small compared to most intensive producers, and he found it increasingly difficult to make a profit. Animal feed rose in price every year, but the price he was getting for his pigs was going down. Supermarkets were demanding cheaper and cheaper meat to supply customers who wanted the lowest prices. James was getting more and more disillusioned. He wished he could walk away, but he knew it would break his father's heart to see him sell the farm.

As he kept the pigs indoors, James leased his land to an agricultural contractor who grew barley for animal feed. James often thought he should work out a deal with this contractor to buy barley for his pigs. But he was tired and had grown complacent, and it was handy to have the feed company deliver and fill his silos once a week.

As soon as James arrived back at the farm, he went to check the pigs. The sow section was all quiet as the piglets suckled. The young gilts, females who haven't had a litter, were noisier and more active. He didn't know any of the pigs, but they knew him. One of the gilts looked up, walked over to her enclosure wall and stretched her neck up curiously.

'Oh-oh, oh-oh, oh,' she chuntered.

James reached in to ruffle her head, but she wasn't used to this behaviour and skittered away, startled.

'Uh-uh-uh-uh-uh,' she grunted.

The other gilts snorted with fright and pressed themselves against the opposite end of the pen. But the gilt that James tried to scratch stood just out of reach, quietly watching him.

James returned the curious gaze of the gilt for an instant, and then he shook himself.

'Get to work, James,' he said to himself. 'No one is going to do it for you.'

He went to check the feed auger, a system of tubes that automated the pig feeding. Next, he sorted out a few issues with machinery in the plant room. Then he closed the shed, locking the big green gates securely on his way out.

He thought of the woman in the agri stores and smiled again. Yes, he'd definitely ask Syl about her the next time he was back.

As he drove down the lane, he saw a donkey standing forlornly at the gate of the neighbouring old cottage. Not for the first time he wondered about him.

10.

Mabel

Mabel had been shocked when James had reached into the pen to touch her. He had never done that before. She was still thinking about his strange behaviour when she was disturbed by a racket going on behind her.

'Stop it! Stop it this minute!' she ordered. 'What's the matter with you all today?'

Hattie, the chief troublemaker, snorted ill-humouredly.

'We're bored!' she exclaimed.

From the beginning, Mabel was the leader of the gilts, and the others relied on her to keep order. All the other gilts looked up to her. She took her job seriously and tried to devise games and distractions to keep them occupied and stop the fighting.

Yet, from some ancestral memory deep inside her, she knew this existence was not normal and longed for freedom. She saw how the sows on the farm, including her mother, lived in a concrete shed their whole life. She knew this was her destiny, and she wasn't happy about it. She saw how the sows were herded into a tiny farrowing crate a week before their piglets were due. In a farrowing crate, they could only stand, and by moving very carefully, they could lie down. It meant they couldn't move around, so they couldn't accidentally squash their piglets.

Mabel's mother had a litter of 14 in the dark early hours one morning. Sows always tend to give birth early in the morning when there are fewer predators. Mabel was the biggest and healthiest female, and James soon earmarked her to stay in the herd.

Mabel and her siblings were all taken from their mother at three weeks and moved into a pen with other litters. Mabel remembered her siblings squealing in panic and her mother crying and pleading with the humans to give her babies back. But the farmers ignored the pigs' distress, and Mabel's mother was moved out of the farrowing pen and straight back in with the boar. And so, in three months, three weeks and three days, she would have another litter of piglets. Then the relentless cycle would begin again, and the sow would be confined for another four weeks in the farrowing crate.

Mabel could see that life for a sow on the farm was a grim and exhausting one. The farmer bred sows twice a year for at least five years, and after giving birth to up to 150 piglets, they were so weak they couldn't have more litters. Then the weary sows, considered useless to the farmer, were soon herded out of the shed. She shuddered at the thought. Everyone knew when pigs left the shed, they were usually on their way to the dreaded abattoir. She even overheard the workers say that the sow's meat was too tough, so it ended up in Germany where they were made into sausages and charcuterie. She was glad the others didn't hear, and she never told anyone what she overheard.

Mabel and her siblings were kept with other litters of piglets the same age until they were five months old, and the farmer would decide their futures. In the meantime, the gilts never got to go outside. They never lay in the sun or felt the rain on their back. They never got to root in soft green grassy fields, find tasty fat morsels of earthworms or slugs or eat crunchy tangy roots. Their world was a concrete floor with central heating and food that automatically came out of a big dispenser into the trough. And they were clever creatures, so they were bored. Really, really bored. They fought a lot, and they bit each other's tails.

Although Mabel, like her mother and grandmother before her, had never lived outside, she had a memory of the outside world. These memories were stirred when she smelled the grass and the plants and the trees on the wind. And when she caught glimpses of the warm rays of sunlight and the showers of soft rain through the open shed door. She also had a strong feeling that she would one day experience all these memories. She didn't know how, but she knew she would.

As part of her efforts to keep the peace and distract the bored gilts, Mabel had become a consummate storyteller. They all loved to listen to her. She told stories about wild pigs from deep in her ancestral memories and helped the others to dream about life beyond their shed.

'Please tell us the story again about how Boarswood got its name?' Hattie begged.

'Yes, do, please,' chorused the rest.

'Quieten down then, and I'll begin,' Mabel replied, and all the gilts settled down as she began to tell her tales.

'Long, long ago, when Ireland was covered in mixed woodland, and wild boar were king, there lived a magnificent boar........'

She told long and epic tales to all the pigs who relaxed into a higgledy-piggledy, clumsy heap around her. Some might have stretched, and a few might have even yawned, but all listened intently to Mabel's words.

Of course, as Mabel retold the stories of Boarswood, she embellished them a bit more each time.

Hattie pig sat up mid-story that day.

'Mabel, that wasn't what you told us the last time,' she said accusingly.

Mabel scowled at her.

'Hattie, do you not remember our mother telling us stories?'

'Of course, I do,' said Hattie.

Mabel gave her a hard glare.

'Well then, you should remember her telling us never to let the truth get in the way of a good story either!'

11.

The Old Cottage

Hugo had a half-day off school. The teachers had a big meeting with the school board and the parish priest, so all the pupils were sent home before lunch break. He was happy. A half-day meant he got to spend a longer time with Honky. The school bus dropped him as usual at his gate. The first thing he saw was Molly smoking in the kitchen, idly waiting for the kettle to boil. She visibly jumped when she saw him.

'I forgot you had a half-day!'

She got up to stub her cigarette out in the sink. Hugo's parents didn't have many rules, but they were clear about not smoking in the house.

'Your sandwich is in the fridge,' she said over her shoulder as she returned to the living room to another quiz show.

Hugo took out his rucksack from under the stairs. He opened the fridge where his dry cheese sandwich was already curling at the edges. He took it all the same and packed it into his lunch box as he knew Honky would like it. Then he grabbed an apple and a banana from the fruit bowl, took some snacks from the biscuit tin, filled his water bottle and packed everything into the rucksack.

He poked his head around the sitting-room door.

'I'm going out. I'll be back at five o'clock.'

He never knew what she understood when he talked.

'Yeah, whatever.'

He could hear her sigh with irritation from the couch.

Hugo took the usual shortcut by hopping over his garden wall into the field beside his family home and passed the office there. He slipped through the hedge and got to the part of the road where the big yew tree grew. As always, he gave the pallet a light rattle, and Honky appeared, her tail wagging fiercely.

'Why don't we explore further and go to that old farmhouse today?' suggested Hugo, pointing to a hill in the distance. 'I don't think anyone lives there.'

Honky did her happy spin, which always brought a smile to Hugo's face.

'You are such a happy creature!'

Honky beamed.

'My friend is here, and we're going off exploring together. So why wouldn't I be happy?'

The two of them took the shortcut into Farmer Herbert's fields. Up they went through Annie's field, slipped around the back of the hen house and slid down the slope into the drain.

They walked further than they ever walked before that day until they reached a stream. It was fast and gurgling, and the rocks were mossy and slippery. They had to find a break in the hedging around Farmer Herbert's fields and take the laneway instead. Finally, they reached the gate to the old cottage on the hill. It was clear the place was long abandoned. The windows were broken, the frames were rotting, and many slates had disappeared off the roof.

A rusty chain hung around the gate. Even though it wasn't locked, Honky went through the gate's bars, and Hugo climbed over them. The cottage door was half open. It had been pushed in, perhaps by one of the cows. Honky saw this as an invitation to enter and trotted straight in, followed by a more cautious Hugo.

The old patterned tiles in the hallway caught Hugo's eye, and he hunkered down and used his fingers to sweep the dust away. The tiles were beautiful, and he began to trace the pattern with his finger. Honky trotted through the first open door and went straight over to the big open fireplace where she started rooting about for exciting smells. A pig's nose is 2,000 times more sensitive than any human nose.

Suddenly, there was a loud whooshing sound, and Honky leapt back as a cloud of soot surrounded her.

'Help! Help!' she cried, although anyone else would have only heard a pig's panicked grunts, which sound something like, 'Uh-uh-uh-uh-uh.'

'What happened? Are you okay?' said Hugo rushing into the room. All he could see was Honky's two wide eyes blinking in all the darkness, and he could just make out a huge pile of twigs and branches in the fireplace.

'It's okay, Honky, honest,' he said. 'You disturbed the fireplace, and an old crow's nest must have tumbled down the chimney.'

'Ooh, I got such a fright, Hugo! said Honky.

Honky never liked being dirty, so she went outside and rolled in the grass until she cleared off most of the soot that covered her.

'I guess we should get back, Honky,' said Hugo. 'It's a long walk back, and I want to get home before my parents do.'

But Honky couldn't resist sticking her snout into the big barn behind the house.

'Let's just have a root about in there, first?' she suggested.

'Be careful,' said Hugo. 'Somebody must be using the barn because the place looks like it's being cared for.'

Hugo followed, and they spent a few minutes looking around. The barn was being used to store big round straw bales and bags of cattle feed, and there were lots of exciting scents for Honky but not much to interest Hugo.

'I have to go, Honky.'

Hugo looked at his wristwatch.

Finally, Honky finished dawdling, and the two companions left the barn. They were walking through the cottage garden when there was a huge screech.

'HEEEEEE-HAAAAAAW! HEEEEEE-HAAAAAAW!'

Honky leapt sideways with fright and bowled into Hugo, sending him flying across the garden.

'Honky, what the heck?' Hugo exclaimed as he struggled back onto his feet.

'What was *THAT*?' said Honky, wide-eyed and trembling.

Hugo saw a long, shaggy head with two tall ears peering around the corner of the cottage.

'THAT, Honky, looks like a donkey!' said the boy.

12.

Mikey

The donkey eyed them both from a safe distance, half-hidden around the side of the cottage. Hugo addressed the shaggy-maned creature with twitching ears: 'Hello there. Apologies if we're trespassing. I'm Hugo, and this is my pal Honky the pig.'

The donkey limped out from behind the shelter of the house. His hooves were curled and twisted, and his coat looked like it needed a good brushing.

'I'm so sorry for frightening you,' the donkey replied. 'I'm Mikey, and I just got excited when I saw you both. Nobody has called here in a long time.'

'Why is that?' asked Hugo.

'I don't know. A man left me here ages ago, and no one has come back since.'

'That's terrible. Is no one looking after you?'

'Not for a long time, but now you two are here!'

The donkey began to tell them the story of how he had been left alone in the fields around the old cottage.

'I lived far away from here and used to carry panniers of turf from the bog all the time,' he said. 'The farm owner had rights on the bog, and every summer, they took me down there and tethered me with the other donkeys in a shady area while the humans cut their turf.'

His eyes glazed over with misty fondness.

'Those were the days. The humans spent the day working, and then around midday, they'd have picnics. And us donkeys spent the day grazing under the alder and willow trees in the cool shade. Then just before sunset, they loaded up our panniers, and we made the journey home. I loved those summer days.

'In winter, I had a small shed at the back of the farmhouse where I could shelter from the rain and the cold. They were good times.'

'So, what happened?' asked Honky.

'The old farmer treated me well. But he got sick, and his nephew took over the farm. He had a big tractor and trailer and said he didn't need a donkey. So, he sold me to a man who gave donkey rides to children on the beach for a living. But then I got lame, and none of the parents would hire me, and they scolded the man and told him he must take me to a vet.'

Mikey explained that was the start of his lonely existence.

'He left me in this field a long time ago, and I haven't seen him since. He heard the owners of the cottage had emigrated to Australia, and he knew no one would pay any attention to a donkey.'

'Gosh, that's so sad,' said Hugo.

'Awful,' agreed Honky, 'and I thought I was lonely!'

'Me too,' said Hugo. 'Does no one stop to talk to you?'

'The cows have been indoors all winter, so they haven't been around for months,' said Mikey. 'Not many pass this way. Farmer Herbert's fields are behind us, and he uses the barn here for storage sometimes. Farmer James owns the next farm. I see them sometimes, but I stay out of their way. I don't like to think where I'll end up next.'

'How do you get food and water?' asked Honky.

'There's plenty to graze on here, and I can go through the hedgerow there, and Farmer Herbert's stream is down the hill.'

'What's wrong with your feet?' said Honky, staring at the donkey's crooked hooves.

'That's a bit rude, Honky!' said Hugo.

Mikey looked down at his curling hooves.

'Don't worry. I know they look terrible. I'm lame because my hooves haven't been trimmed for years. It's so painful that I must lie down a lot of the time, which is fine when it's warm and sunny but not very pleasant in the winter. Donkeys don't have a waterproof coat, so we suffer in cold wet climates, you know.'

'I'm so sorry,' said Hugo.

'Oh, it's not so bad. Mustn't complain. I'm lucky because I could push in the door to the cottage, so I can shelter in bad rain.'

Suddenly, Hugo remembered his packed lunch.

'Here, look what I have!'

He reached into his schoolbag and presented the apple for Mikey and the sandwich and the banana for Honky. Honky snaffled the banana complete with the peel in seconds. Hugo was unwrapping a biscuit bar for himself when he heard the low heavy rumble of a lorry approaching.

'It's one of the trucks coming to collect Farmer James' pigs,' said the donkey, sadly. 'I watch the lorries arrive empty and leave full as they go to the abattoir.'

Honky, like every animal on the farm, had heard about the dreaded abattoirs. No one was exactly sure what happened in these places, but they knew for sure that no one who went there ever came back.

'I can see the pigs' eyes and the terror in them as they pass,' Mikey said, his long nose flaring at the memory. 'It's a terrible thing. I can smell the fear from every lorry that passes.'

Honky visibly shivered when she heard this, and Hugo became even paler than usual.

'The pigs have terrible lives on that farm,' added Mikey. 'I've talked to the chickens from there, and they say they're never let out of their big concrete shed.'

Hugo's eyebrows drew together, and his smooth forehead creased into a frown.

'That's not right, is it Honky?'

'Not right at all!' said Honky with passion. 'What can we do?'

'We need to get on that farm and talk to the pigs. That way, we'll find out what's going on.'

'I'll help if I can,' said Mikey.

Hugo had a thought.

'You can be our head of surveillance! You're perfectly positioned on the lane to tell us what time the lorries come and go and what times the farmer leaves. It'll be safer for us to go and investigate if we have that information.'

Honky's tail wagged in happy agreement, and Mikey's chest filled with pride and a new sense of purpose.

'I can do that!' he said.

'We have a plan!' said Honky.

'But when will you come back?' said Mikey, suddenly scared that the boy and the pig might never return.

'We'll be back tomorrow, won't we Honky? And I'll try to work out how to fix Mikey's hooves.'

Mikey's top lip curled up, and he threw his head back and emitted a loud 'HEEEEEE-HAAAAAW' before he could stop himself,

Both Hugo and Honky laughed.

'Isn't this great?' said Hugo. 'We had no friends a couple of weeks ago, and now we all have two friends.'

Hugo laughed, and Honky and Mikey snorted and brayed in delighted agreement.

13.

New Shoes

Hugo and Honky went to see Mikey most days after school finished. Mikey was always thrilled to see them coming and continued watching the comings and goings on the farm next door.

Spring arrived suddenly, and the weather got warmer and dryer. Farmers let their cows out into fields again. They began trundling up and down the lanes, roads and fields in their tractors and trailers, spreading slurry and checking their stock daily. It never seemed safe to go to the farm.

Meanwhile, Hugo and Honky got increasingly worried about Mikey, who was limping around the farm in agony by now.

'We have to do something, Hugo,' said Honky one day as they went home through the fields. 'It's getting worse by the day. Mikey can hardly walk at all now.'

'I'll try to think of something, Honky.'

But Hugo was stumped. He had no money for a vet, and his parents wouldn't help. They would be horrified to hear he was hanging around a derelict house with a pig and a lame donkey. Then a thought came to him – *the school library!* He went to the school library, and sure enough, he found a book on horse care. He pulled down the book and looked up the chapter on caring for hooves. He read how a blacksmith uses a rasp, a tool like a giant nail file for filing down a horse's foot, and he studied the picture of the blacksmith using the device.

Hugo raced home after school and rummaged through the toolbox in the garage that the previous owners had left behind. He found something like the rasp he saw in the book and another sharp-looking implement that he thought might work. That afternoon, Hugo and Honky wore big smiles on their faces and carried the two big tools as they arrived to see Mikey.

'We're going to give you new shoes, Mikey,' said Hugo, dragging out an old woodworm-riddled box that he found in the barn. 'Honky you stand here, and let Mikey lean up against the wall there.'

They both did what they were told.

'Lift your front foot Mikey and put it on this box.'

Mikey did so, but wobbled badly on three bad legs.

'Honky can you lean against Mikey to give him a bit of support?'

Hugo set to work with the rasp. Honky found it hard because it was hot and horse flies landed on her and bit her. She jumped and squealed a couple of times as they nipped.

'Honky, for heaven's sake, keep still!'

'I can't when I'm being eaten alive!'

Slowly, Hugo managed to pare off much of the rough parts of Mikey's feet. Finally, when he had done all four, he stood back and said, 'Mikey, walk around a bit and see how that feels.'

'Yes, it's a bit better.'

'Okay,' said Hugo. 'It's working. Come back, and I'll do a bit more.'

He kept at them for another hour, stopping only to have a swig of water from his water bottle.

'That's the best I can do for now. That other clippers I brought down is blunt and useless. Try walking on the concrete around the barn to help smooth the rough edges, Mikey.'

Instead, Mikey set off doing laps. The donkey was delighted with himself. For the first time in ages, walking and running wasn't agony, and his friends cheered him on as he hee-hawed in delight.

14.

The Horror

With the warm weather, the lane got busier, and the three friends stayed behind the cottage so the farmers wouldn't spot them.

'It's going to be difficult to get into that farm now,' said Mikey, with a shake of his head.

Hugo sighed.

'It's getting harder to get here too without being seen.'

'We're always ducking into gateways and hedges to hide,' added Honky.

The three friends decided to forget about the pigs on the farm down the lane that day. Instead, they spent the next few hours in blissful peace. The sun was shining; the birds were making nests and flying overhead with clumps of sheep wool that they found caught on barbed wire fencing. Mikey was happily grazing. Honky was sniffing and rooting, and Hugo was poking about in the old cottage.

Suddenly, the sound of clanging, banging and commotion filled the air. There was the roar of an engine and much high-pitched squealing, and Mikey looked up startled. Hugo ran to the front door, and Honky charged past him.

'Wuh-wuh, wuh-wuh, wuh!' she snorted. 'What's going on? What's happening?'

Just at that moment, a big lorry trundled past the gate. It had ventilation slits all along the sides, and Hugo could see eyes peering out and snouts poking through. The sound of grunts and squeals filled the air, but the terrible smell was all-embracing. It seemed to settle and linger in a gelatinous layer on everything.

Hugo even gagged. He was much more sensitive to smell than other children, and strong odours unsettled him.

'What was that, Mikey?' said Hugo when the lorry passed.

'That's one of the lorries collecting the pigs. I told you it's awful.'

Hugo's shoulders slumped with the weight of his guilt.

'We've waited too long. I'm not waiting any longer. I'm going to try and see what's going on now. Honky are you coming with me?'

Honky was always ready for an adventure.

'Can you keep a lookout, Mikey?' she said. 'If anyone comes down the lane towards us, call us. Everyone can hear your hee-haw for miles!'

Honky and Hugo started to walk down the lane slowly and tentatively, ready to leap into the hedge or a gateway if they heard anything coming. The noise of squealing and banging got louder as they approached a set of tall green gates. The pair ducked in behind one of the concrete piers where they had a clear view through the gates, but they couldn't be seen.

The noise was so loud that Hugo clamped his palms to his ears and rocked back and forth. Honky watched as a big lorry backed up to a ramp. Four men wielding sticks and wearing overalls and wellies stood on either side of the ramp, herding loads and loads of dirty and scared squealing pigs into the back of the lorry. Honky shivered as he watched the men bang the sides of the shed with their sticks.

'Hup! Hup! Hup!' they yelled at the pigs.

The smell was even worse than the noise. Honky and Hugo had never smelled anything so bad.

Hugo whispered to Honky.

'This is just awful. I think I'm going to be sick.'

Honky looked up at Hugo in alarm.

'Well, don't be sick on me! We have to get out of here before we are seen. I don't want to be beaten up that ramp as well.'

She nudged Hugo to get him to move, and they ran back down the lane, keeping close to the hedges in case they needed to hide.

They were shaken when they got back to the little cottage. The happy mood from earlier had dissipated, and now everyone was sombre. Hugo wondered aloud why so many pigs were living in that shed and why they smelled so bad.

'Us pigs are clean creatures,' Honky insisted. 'We don't smell, and we certainly don't make that much noise for no reason.'

Hugo was upset by the noises he heard too.

'Those pigs were very distressed. I know now what you meant, Mikey. I could see the fear in their eyes too.'

Mikey nudged Hugo with his wet nose, and Hugo wrapped his arms around him and buried his face into his soft, fluffy mane.

'I didn't only see the fear; I could smell it,' said Honky almost to herself. 'I never want to see that place again.'

The three stood in silence for a while, but when Hugo looked up, his face was a picture of resolve.

'Well, I'm going back to that place. I have to do something, Honky, and this time, I'm not delaying. I'm going back tomorrow.'

Hugo is nuts, thought Honky. *The smell almost made him sick, and he can't bear the noise, but he still wants to back?*

But she shrugged.

'Well, if you're going, I guess that means I'm going too.'

'And I guess I'll keep lookout,' said Mikey.

Honky and Hugo soon started the long walk back home through the fields. They were both quiet and thoughtful and hardly exchanged a word.

'Have you got a plan, Hugo?'

'Not yet, Honky.'

At the yew tree, Hugo said goodbye to Honky. He crossed the field beside his house, and a woman working in the office waved out the window. But Hugo was too busy thinking about the horror of what he'd seen.

15.

Annie & James

Annie searched through her fields the following day and discovered the gap that Honky's siblings were using to escape into Farmer Herbert's farm. Even though it was lashing rain, she managed to fix the hole and attached the new bigger battery, so there was much stronger power surging through the electric fencing now.

'There now, you little divils. Try and get through that now!' she said, satisfied with her work.

Now, maybe, I won't have to deal with grumpy Farmer Herbert again for a while, she thought with relief.

But later that afternoon, Annie bumped into another farmer that she wanted to avoid. She was walking down the village's main street in between showers when she spotted the man from the agri store.

She blushed as she saw the look of amused recognition on the man's face.

Oh yes, I'm that woman who flung herself into your arms, she thought, but she returned a bright smile all the same.

'How are you doing?' he asked.

'Fine, thanks. Apologies for yesterday. My mind was on escaping pigs.'

'You keep pigs?'

'Yes, but just a few free range. A bit too free range really!'

She explained that she was rushing in before the agri store closed to get a new battery to contain her 'free-range' pigs.

'It's a shame you rushed off so,' he said. 'I could have told you that you probably didn't need a new battery. The earth rods for the fence may not be buried deep enough. They have to be buried in wet ground to get good contact and conduct a big enough shock. If you get that right, the pigs will soon stop being so cheeky, and that'll be the end of them trying for gaps or ducking under the fence.'

'Well, maybe, you could call in one day when you are passing. It's always good to get another perspective on what I'm doing.'

'I'll be delighted to. I'm James, by the way.'

'I'm Annie,' she replied, and they shook hands.

James smiled and had gone on his way before she realised she hadn't even told him where she lived. But Annie was used to life in the country now. She remembered back to when she had first moved to the area and had gone to buy a coal delivery. After she paid for the coal, she waited patiently for the shop assistant to come back and get her address. Eventually, the girl came back to her.

'Are you okay? Do you need anything else?'

'Do you not need to take my address?'

The girl looked at her oddly.

'Well, it's the Jeffrey place, isn't it?'

Annie soon realised that everyone knew everyone, and they even knew blow-ins like her.

When she got home from the village, she checked in the vegetable patch and found Honky snuggled up in her bed, which was unusual these days. Annie didn't see much of Honky now. Her favourite little red pig wasn't hanging around the farm and trailing after her like she usually did. Annie checked on Honky's siblings and found them in their pen, snorting in disgruntlement.

'Yes, that fence has put a halt to your gallop, hasn't it?' she said. 'And I guess that's where Honky has been disappearing to as well. She's been out in Farmer Herbert's fields with you lot, hasn't she?' Annie thought she had it all worked out.

16.

The Farm

Hugo's grand plans were ruined that day. He had been determined to return to the farm when there were no lorries there. Mikey said the lorries only came once a week at most, so he knew it should be safe.

But he watched the rain lash against his classroom window all day long, and when Hugo got home from school, Molly the minder said he was not allowed out.

'Your mother would kill me for letting you out in this, especially when you were off school for a week with bronchitis!' she said. 'Go on up to your room and do your homework for a change.'

Over at Annie's farm, Honky looked out her woodshed that morning and decided the weather wasn't fit for man or beast and went back to bed. She felt sure that Hugo wouldn't arrive, and if he did, she'd hear him anyway. Moreover, she was tired of trying to make sense of what she'd witnessed the day before. So, she snuggled down in her big straw bed in the woodshed and stayed there all day.

The next morning was Saturday, and Hugo rose early and got dressed. Molly didn't work on weekends, and his parents liked to sleep in late. His mother usually got up at some stage to make a pot of tea. She loaded up a tray with teacups, sugar, milk and the newspaper that arrived in the letterbox, and she took it upstairs. But she let Hugo make his own breakfast and watch television and never worried about him because, normally, he never did anything at weekends. Until he met Honky and Mikey, he didn't do much during the week either. Hugo knew that his parents would spend the rest of the day in the study. He believed they didn't care what he did, as long as it didn't interfere with their work. His parents took their work very seriously indeed. He slipped down the stairs, closed the front door softly and took off down the field at the back of his house.

Honky heard Hugo rattling the pallet and whistling. The dogs heard him too and started barking in the house. Honky could hear Annie shouting at them to be quiet.

'You're early,' said Honky, delighted to see his friend.

'It's Saturday,' said Hugo. 'I've no school, so we can spend most of the day together.'

'I'm glad it's a Saturday so, but I don't keep track of the days,' said Honky. 'Every day is fun day for me except the other day.'

'I can't stop thinking about those pigs either,' Hugo said.

Annie still hadn't spotted the escape route under the fence at the back of the hen house, so they took off through Farmer Herbert's fields as usual.

'I'd say poor Mikey is fed up we didn't come down yesterday,' said Hugo. 'It was such a terrible day, so I hope he managed to get in the doorway to shelter.'

Hugo waved as soon as he saw Mikey's head sticking out over the gate. He was waiting for them. As soon as he saw his two friends arriving, he gave a big delighted 'HEEEEEE-HAAAAAW.' Hugo had brought another banana for Honky and an apple for Mikey from the fruit bowl in the kitchen.

He watched Honky devour the banana, skin and all. Hugo thought most sayings about pigs are true. *Eat like a pig – that's definitely true,* he thought. He had seen Honky eating. She loved her food. She was a bit messy, but so would he if he used his mouth and didn't have two hands and cutlery to help.

Stubborn as a pig - true too, he thought. Honky was pig-headed at times and only did things she wanted to do. Honky was a pain sometimes to get moving. She liked to do things in her own time.

But dirty as a pig - not true at all, he thought. By being around Honky, he knew pigs are the cleanest of all animals. She said she only like rolling in mud when it's hot.

'Pigs don't have sweat glands like humans,' Honky explained. 'So, covering ourselves in wet mud cools us down. Pigs, especially pink ones, suffer terribly from sunburn and a mud bath protects their skin too.'

Honky finished her banana with a satisfied burp.

'Well, what's the plan then, Hugo?'

'We go back to the farm,' he said simply.

Mikey was worried.

'There are no lorries today, but Farmer James hasn't left today, so he's somewhere on the farm,' he said. 'Be careful out there.'

17.

The Concrete Prison

It took a few seconds for Honky to see in the dark. But it took far less for the smell to hit her snout. It was horrific. There were rows of concrete pens with drainage slits on the floor. Each pen had a concrete wall around it with a long trough at one end. There must have been twenty pigs in each pen, but they were so small they could hardly turn in them. Their tails were cut off, and the pigs were covered in their own poo. Some of them had bites and were bleeding.

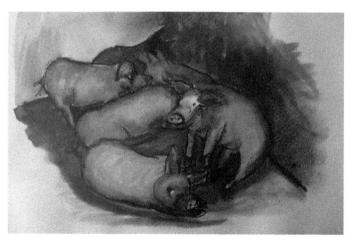

'It's like a giant, smelly concrete prison,' whispered Hugo.

The two approached one small pen and peered in the gate. The pigs stared back at them with lifeless eyes. Honky made her greeting sounds, 'ha-ha, ha-ha, ha' and was shocked when none of the pigs responded.

'It's like they don't understand pig language or etiquette,' she said, her eyes wide.

She saw Hugo put his hand slowly through the bars of the gate and witnessed the pigs jump back in fear.

'Hey, piggies, I'm your friend,' Hugo whispered. 'I'd never harm you.'

One of the pigs took a step closer.

'How do we know that?' she said. 'Humans have never been kind to us before.'

Honky was relieved. *At last, a response!*

'You just haven't met the right humans,' Honky replied. 'This is my friend Hugo, and he's a friend to all pigs.'

She came closer again and looked quizzically at them.

'I'm Mabel and I'm in charge here. Nice to meet you both. Ha-ha, ha-ha, ha.'

Finally - normal pig talk, thought Honky.

As Honky started to chat with Mabel, Hugo walked deeper into the shed to investigate more and soon disappeared into the gloom.

'Where do you go to sleep?' asked Honky, looking around at all the pigs packed in the concrete pen.

'What do you mean?' asked Mabel.

'Well, I have a deep bed of straw in my woodshed. My boss, Annie, makes it up for me under the oil tank.'

'Oh,' replied Mabel. 'We just sleep here, wherever we can lie.'

'Does the farmer not make a straw bed for you?' Honky asked incredulously.

'What's straw?' asked Mabel.

'Wow, Mabel, I think we have a lot to teach you!'

Mabel introduced Honky to all the other gilts. Honky was aghast to discover Mabel and the others had never been outside. They didn't even know grass, never mind straw.

'Have you ever thought about escaping?' Honky asked.

'All the time,' they chorused. 'Mabel tells us stories about our ancestors, the wild boar who lived in the woods here when we were the kings.'

Hugo reappeared, shaking his head.

'I've had a good walk around,' he said, addressing Honky. 'There are poor mother pigs squashed into tiny cages at the other end, and their babies are all running around them. There is a huge boar as well. He told me he is called Len.'

'Ah yes, Len is a bit gruff, but he's a nice pig underneath it all,' said Mabel.

Hugo looked nervously out the open door of the shed. They managed to enter through a side door that was left unlocked.

'We better get going, Honky, before some of the workers arrive,' he said. 'We don't want to get caught trespassing, or we'll find it hard to get back here again.'

Honky turned to Mabel.

'We can come tomorrow morning early again,' she said. 'It seems to be a good time to come, and we can talk more.'

Honky and Hugo made their way back to the cottage unseen. They reported everything they had seen to Mikey.

'I didn't expect it would be a pig paradise, and I was right,' he sighed.

They stayed for a while, but Hugo kept glancing at his watch.

'Let's go Honky,' he said. 'I need to get back home before my parents discover I'm gone. It might be the one day they decide to check on me, and I don't want to arouse their suspicions.'

But Honky was always difficult to get moving. She liked to do things in her own time, and she was happy snuffling in the garden and chatting to Mikey.

Hugo became lost in thought as he waited for her. If Honky had asked, he would have told her he was thinking about designing a proper pig farm. In his mind, he was creating a place where pigs had a cosy, warm place to sleep and a shady, grassy area outdoors to root. He thought about installing a mud wallow to cool down on hot days and even a pool for the piglets to play in.

He jumped when Honky suddenly nudged him. 'Hurry up, Hugo!' She decided she was ready and it was time to go.

18.

The Plan

Later that evening, Honky wandered around. Her brothers and sister were fenced into Annie's top field now. They hadn't been able to get back into Farmer Herbert's meadows and were fed up.

'It's okay for you,' moaned Stumpy. 'You can go where you like. It's not fair!'

'If you saw the conditions other pigs live in, you wouldn't complain,' said Honky.

Her mind was working furiously. What if she and Hugo freed the pigs in the concrete shed? Would it be possible? She knew they couldn't manage on their own as the wild pigs did, though. They'd need shelter and food, and water.

I need to talk to Hugo about it, she thought. *Hugo goes to school, so he's clever. He'll come up with an idea.*

She suddenly realised she was tired, so she went for a rest in her woodshed. She found the fat cat sitting on the oil tank there.

'Good evening,' said Honky, but the cat only looked disdainfully at her.

Honky started to make her bed. Like all pigs, she liked to make a fresh bed before she got into it. She loosened up all the straw with her snout, and using her powerful neck, she tossed it in the air. Then she pushed it up against the wall as a cushion to lie against. Finally, when it was all nice and comfortable, she lay down head and elbows first and her bum and back legs following.

Honky fell into a deep sleep and was having a lovely dream when she was disturbed. She woke with a fright to see Hugo standing above her in the half-light.

'You startled me, Hugo,' she gasped. 'What are you doing here in the middle of the night?'

'It's not the middle of the night, Honky. It's early morning,' said Hugo.

'Now, shove over,' he added as he sat on the straw with his back against the wall and his long legs sticking out under the oil tank stand.

'I couldn't stop thinking about those poor pigs,' he said. 'And I think I have an idea.'

'I was hoping that you'd have an idea!' said Honky, feeling delighted and excited at once.

Hugo started telling Honky his plan, and she listened intently. He had thought of everything. His plan was daring, and if they could pull it off, it would be incredible.

Everything centred around the derelict cottage where Mikey lived. The big barn on the farm was filled with big round straw bales. Hugo had also spotted a pallet of cattle nuts in the corner, which they could use to feed the pigs. The fields behind were Farmer Herbert's and sloped down to a copse of trees and that stream full of cold, clear water.

'We can get the pigs down the lane and lead them down the fields, and they can live under the trees by the water,' said Hugo. 'It's perfect. We can take down the straw bales for bedding and drag down a bag of nuts a day to feed them. There are 30 bags on the pallet, so in theory, we have enough for a month.'

Honky remembered the cows grazing on the other side of the stream.

'Yes, but there aren't many trees, and Farmer Herbert is sure to spot the pigs when he arrives to bring the cows in for milking,' said Honky.

'Well, the pigs can come up the fields before he arrives and hide behind the back of the barn,' said Hugo. 'Farmer Herbert is like clockwork. Mikey has been watching for days now, and he knows the exact time Farmer Herbert goes to collect the cows for morning milking and what time he lets them back into the field. It's the same routine morning and evening. And Farmer Herbert rarely ever comes to the shed. When he does, he comes down the lane on his quad bike. That's quite loud, and Mikey knows the sound of it, so he can warn everyone.'

Honky felt like squealing in delight.

'The rest of the day, the pigs can use the field and shelter under the trees and use the stream for water and for wallowing in!' she said.

'Yes, and if the weather turns really bad, they can shelter in the barn,' said Hugo.

Honky gasped in admiration.

'Hugo, you are a genius!'

'I'm not Honky. It's very risky, and to be honest, even if everything goes to plan, we only have enough food for a month, and how long will it be before we are discovered?'

The pair sat in silence, chewing over the idea. They knew it wasn't a long-term solution by any means, but it was a start. The pigs would have a chance to experience life outside a concrete shed for the first time in their lives. Honky had often heard Annie saying to herself, 'all good things come to those who wait.' At the time Honky didn't know what Annie meant, but now she thought she might.

'We have to plan this carefully and think of every possible thing that could go wrong,' said Hugo.

'I think we should talk to Mabel now,' said Honky. 'The pigs have to be ready too.'

'Good idea,' said Hugo. 'It's Sunday, so there probably won't be anyone about.'

They made their way quickly up through the fields and down the lane to the old cottage. Mikey was delighted to see them so early.

The two shared their plans for the great escape.

'That's super!' he said. 'And I can help herd the piglets up the lane.'

But Hugo was a boy in a hurry.

'I need to check out the entire shed, Honky. We can't rely on the side door to get all the pigs out. It will be too much of a crush and will slow us down.'

He was already heading for the lane.

'Hold on,' said Honky. 'I need to share our plans with Mabel.'

But Hugo went over the cottage gate and vanished up the lane towards the big green gates. Honky trundled along after him, enjoying a sniff here and a snuffle there. There was no way she would try to keep up with Hugo when he was in this determined mood. When Honky reached the farm gates, she slipped under and found the side door already open.

Mabel saw her coming and gave her a great greeting. She was delighted to see Honky, and her eyes widened in wonderment when she heard the plan for the escape.

'Well, what do you think?' said Honky.

'I think it's amazing,' she said, tears filling her eyes. 'We have a chance for freedom at last!'

But Mabel quickly pulled herself together. She was the boss. She had to get organised.

'I'll get the word around to the others, and we'll await your instructions.'

Meanwhile, Hugo had walked the length of the shed. Len, the boar, pointed out the big red lever that opened the roller doors leading to the loading bay. This was where the lorries reversed and dropped their ramp to load the pigs for the abattoir.

Hugo spotted a ladder in the corner, and leaning it against a wall, he climbed it to the top so that he could survey the shed. From that position, he counted the pens to work out the sequence for releasing the pigs. He would pull on the big red lever and open the doors to the loading bay.

He had to release the gilts and Mabel, who were in the first few pens. Next were the sow pens, then the farrowing crate pens with the sows and their piglets. The farrowing crates would be the trickiest. They all had to be opened individually. He wasn't worried about the piglets because he knew they would follow their mothers, but unlocking all those small pens would take more time. The longer he and Honky spent in the place, the greater the chance they would be discovered. The boar pen with Len and the other male weaners was located at the end of the shed.

He would open the roller doors for the pigs and when all the pigs were out, he would close the doors, run back through the shed and leave by the side door. That way, the doors would be closed and wouldn't arouse suspicion. They would station Mikey at the green gates where he would wait until the last pig came out, would bring up the rear and round up any slow pigs. Then Hugo would shut the green gates and run to catch up with Honky at the front. Mable should be in the middle passing back any information.

Yes, Hugo thought. *We have a plan, and it just might work.*

19.

The Date is Set

In truth, Mikey was worried. He wanted to see the plan succeed and wanted the pigs to lead a normal life, but what about him? If the pigs were discovered on the farm, it would draw attention to him. The farmers might take him away, and what would become of him then? He was old, and few farmers needed a donkey now. Since he had made friends with Honky and Hugo, his life at the old cottage had become so much better. Now Mikey feared his time at the cottage might soon be over. Hugo couldn't help notice that Mikey looked sad.

'What's wrong, Mikey?'

'I feel a bit worried, Hugo.'

'Why, Mikey?'

'I'm worried what will happen to me after all this.'

Hugo smiled.

'I have a secret,' he said. 'I have a plan for you too!'

Hugo had been thinking a lot about what would become of Mikey, and he had a brainwave. His house was situated on a big plot of land that was part of a larger field originally. The previous owners had treated it as a garden and kept the grass cut short. But Hugo's parents had no interest in gardening and had let it go wild.

Hugo knew his father had done a deal with Farmer Farrelly nearby, who suggested that he cut the grass on their site and add it to his silage. Knowing that Hugo's father was a 'townie', the canny farmer agreed to do this for 'a very reasonable cost'. Hugo's father agreed to pay him every year to cut it.

'My father shouldn't be paying anything, so I'm going to suggest they move you in to keep the grass cut instead,' said Hugo. 'You can use the garage at the back of the house for shelter because my parents never use it for their cars or anything. They only store the bins there. What do you think of that? We could see each other every day then, and when we get you into my garden, I will get my father to ring a proper blacksmith so you'll have hooves to be proud of!'

Mikey thought this was a fantastic idea and gave a giant 'HEEEEEE-HAAAAAW' in celebration.

'Oh Hugo, I've been so worried,' he said. 'I was afraid you and Honky might think I was being selfish and thinking about myself if I mentioned it.'

'I wouldn't have thought that in a million years, Mikey, and neither would Honky! We know you have a heart of gold, and we are a band of brothers now.'

Hugo paused.

'Well, I suppose Honky is a girl, but you know what I mean,' he said.

Honky, startled by Mikey's loud braying, rushed over.

'What's all the excitement? What am I missing?'

So, Hugo explained what they had been talking about, and Honky did her happy spin and fell over.

'Oh, that will be fantastic!' she exclaimed when she caught her breath again. 'And we'll all live close to each other then - we can see each other every day!'

Hugo asked his two friends to settle down and think.

'Guys, we need to get serious and make our final plans for the great escape.'

He really liked the sound of 'the great escape.' He wondered how long it would take to release all the pigs and get them all up the lane and down the fields to the stream. Honky could move at the speed of a greyhound when she wanted to, but that didn't happen very often. Hugo knew they would need to get the pigs up the lane and under cover of the trees by the stream as fast as possible. If anyone spotted them on the route, the game was up. It might work if they moved the pigs very early one morning.

Thank goodness, it's light now before 5.00am, he thought.

Honky could see the concentration lines on Hugo's brow as he thought about their next moves.

'What are you thinking, Hugo?' Honky asked.

'I think it will have to be early on a Sunday morning, and this Sunday coming should be it.'

'That soon?' said Honky, a bit shocked.

'The sooner, the better, I think,' said Hugo. 'Because if we think about it too long, we might get cold feet. And we don't want to delay in case more lorries arrive.'

Honky and Mikey shuddered at the thought of the lorries and agreed.

When Honky got home and squeezed behind the yew tree pallet, she spotted Annie and a strange man looking over the fence at her brothers and sister in the top field. She watched as they walked down to the stables and vanished from sight.

Who's that man? she wondered. *I haven't seen him around here before.*

She started making her bed and was tossing the straw around when Annie and the man appeared in front of her.

'James, this is the piglet I was telling you about. Well, she's not really a piglet anymore, but her name is Honky.'

James…, thought Honky. *He must be Farmer James!*

Honky watched and listened as Annie started telling this strange man all about her. She could tell by the man's bewildered expression that he thought she should be locked up in one of his concrete pens.

'Do you just leave her loose about the place?' he asked, almost aghast.

'I do,' replied Annie. 'Honky's been free to come and go where she pleases since I moved her out of the house. She just hangs around the garden and part of the top field. I often worry that she must be a bit lonely, but she seems happy enough.'

Harrumph! thought Honky. *If only she knew. Now, what is lovely Annie doing with horrible Farmer James?*

Annie asked if he would like a cup of tea, and Honky saw them turn and walk back to the house. Honky fumed, watching the house. They stayed in there for ages; far too long for Honky's liking.

20.

The Long Wait

The week dragged by. Every day after school, Hugo called over for Honky, and they went over to Mikey. Every day, they also crept in to see Mabel and the pigs.

Mabel was quivering with excitement, and all the pigs were oinking and grunting non-stop about the great escape. There had been no squabbling for days.

'It's unbelievable,' said Mabel. 'Not a row in days, and that has never happened before. We're all working as a team for once.'

Len was totally in support of the scheme. He warned all the troublemakers that Hugo was the boss, and whatever he ordered them to do, they better do it or suffer the consequences. Naturally, none of them wanted to get on the wrong side of Len. He had huge tusks and weighed over 400 kilos. He was a gentle boar behind it all, but he had to present himself as a tough guy to keep order among the male weaners.

Len could hardly dare believe that he and his herd might soon be free. For years, he dreamt about freedom too. When he slept, he ran through cool dark woods, and his legs would furiously gallop even as he lay on his side. He could almost smell the sweet scent of roots and fallen chestnuts and taste the fresh grass. He loved when he caught sight of sun rays shining in the window above his concrete run. He stretched out and dreamt about deep wallows and shady dens.

Like Honky, he couldn't keep track of the days, but he knew the day was coming closer and closer as the anticipation and excitement built up.

'Are you coming in the morning?' asked Mabel for the fourth time this week.

'No, we coming in three mornings time,' replied Hugo patiently.

'We will be here at five o'clock in the morning when it is just getting bright, and we have to have you all down behind the barn by six. We must wait for Farmer Herbert to finish milking his cows, but he should have them back in the field by eight. Then we can all move down the fields to the stream. He doesn't always even come into the field. Normally, he just opens the electric fence, and the cows are always waiting in an orderly line for him. But Mikey saw him drive his quad bike down to the stream last week, and if he looked across the stream, he would easily spot you all, so we can't take that chance.'

The planning, anticipation and talking went on for the next couple of days. The piglets were warned there was to be no squealing. The gilts were warned there was no biting. The more sensible pigs were given the task of spreading the straw and organising the feed.

The following Saturday, Hugo was quiet and thoughtful when he met with Honky and Mikey. He brought the rasp and clippers and worked on filing Mikey's hooves again.

'We need you to be fast on your feet tomorrow, Mikey!' he said.

Then he oiled the old rusting cottage gate so that Mikey could be let out without the squeaking hinges alerting anyone.

Afterwards, he sat down with his back to the cottage wall and hugged his knees with his arms. Honky sat down beside him.

'You're miles away,' she said. 'Are you nervous about tomorrow?'

'I am. I don't think I will sleep a wink tonight,' confessed Hugo.

Mikey assured his friends he'd be ready by the cottage gate at first light, and Honky and Hugo set off back up the lane in silence. It wasn't until they were almost home that Honky spoke.

'Hugo, what if it all goes wrong and the pigs run off all over the place, or someone spots us?'

'Don't think about things like that. Think positively. We have spent ages planning this, and we have Mabel, Len and Mikey to help. It's got to work, Honky. For all our sakes.'

21.

The Great Escape

Hugo woke up and jumped out of bed, his heart beating fast. He could hardly believe he had slept. It was 4.15am, and the first streaks of light had appeared in the sky. He dressed hurriedly and crept downstairs. He stuffed some fruit and biscuit bars into his bag and filled his water bottle.

By the time he reached Honky, she was already up and pacing around nervously.

'Come on, Hugo. Let's go!' she whispered.

They walked quickly down Farmer Herbert's fields, faster than they ever had in the past. Finally, they slipped out onto the lane to avoid the stream and spotted Mikey as they approached the cottage. He had his head over the gate and was looking up and down anxiously.

'All quiet,' he whispered. 'No one is stirring.'

Hugo opened the gate for Mikey and closed it again. He didn't want to do anything to draw attention to the cottage. The last thing they needed was some farmer to notice the open gates as he trundled down the lane on his tractor. They set off for Farmer James' big green gates, ready to fling themselves into the shadows of the hedgerows if they heard anything approach.

Hugo looked at the big gates.

'I think we should leave them closed for now until all the pigs are out of the pen – just in case,' he whispered.

Honky and Mikey nodded in agreement.

Honky slipped through the gate while Hugo climbed over it, and the two entered the shed through the unlocked side door. Honky went straight to Mabel. She had been pacing for the past hour and snapping at the gilts as they quizzed her impatiently.

'Mabel, where are they?'

'Mabel, is it much longer now?'

'Mabel, when can we go?'

Hugo strode quickly and lightly to the end of the shed to release Len first.

'Morning Len!' he whispered cheerily.

'Morning,' replied Len. 'Where do you want me to go?'

'We'll need you to keep order,' Hugo said as he climbed over the wall into the farrowing pens. He began flicking open the bolts on the crates, and one by one, the trapped sows stood up and stretched their cramped limbs.

'Loosen up by walking around while Hugo releases the other pigs,' Len instructed.

When the gilts from the pen next to Mabel's began to jump about skittishly, Len growled at them, and they quickly quietened down.

Hugo went through the entire shed, releasing all the pigs as he went, and Len instructed them to form an orderly and silent queue at the loading bay doors.

'Hey, stop shoving me,' squealed an older sow to one of the younger gilts.

'I'm not. Someone is pushing me, and they pushed me into you,' replied Hattie.

'Settle down, you lot,' growled Len under his breath. 'Do you want this to succeed or not? If you don't all cooperate, you may as well go back into your pens.'

There was a bit of a melee when the piglets got mixed up following their mothers.

'Sqweee, sqweee, sqweeeeeeee......,' they called to the sows.

'Chunter, chunter, chunter,' replied their mothers.

Finally, every pig was out and waiting in line patiently at the big roller doors.

Mabel approached Honky.

'If you raise a trotter, that's the signal for all of us to stop and try and hide,' she said.

'Roger, that,' said Honky, who was starting to feel very important.

'Who's Roger?' said Mabel.

Honky giggled.

'Never mind. I'll tell you again.'

Hugo climbed the ladder to double-check no one was left behind in any of the pens.

'Right, this is what I'm going to do now. Are you all listening?'

A murmur rumbled through the herd like the Mexican wave, and even in the dim light, he could see them all nodding in unison.

'I'm going to open the roller doors, and you are all to file out slowly and stay there quietly until Honky gives you the order to move.'

'Is everyone clear?'

They all nodded in unison.

Hugo reached up and pulled the big red lever. Slowly the doors rumbled and shuddered and began to lift. Honky was standing at the front, and she led them out. Len was at the back, and Mikey watched from the gates.

It only took a few minutes for all the pigs to get out, but it felt like an hour to Hugo standing by the big red lever. Finally, when Len was out, Hugo pushed the lever again, and the doors started to rumble downwards. He ran out the side door to the green gates.

'All clear,' said Mikey, and Hugo opened the gates.

Some younger pigs scattered to a hedge and rooted about, calling to each other.

'Come over here! Smell this! Wow!'

'Here, take a bite of this! It's delicious!'

The older pigs were looking around, blinking in the early morning light. Meanwhile, the piglets were running around in chaotic and excited circles as their mothers desperately tried to keep them under control.

Hugo gave the thumbs up to Honky, who began to lead everyone out the gate. The pigs all trailed after her, following her instructions to keep close to the hedge. Mabel and Len moved up and down the line, herding everyone and snapping at pigs found dallying with their snout in the hedgerows.

Hugo waited for the hundreds of pigs to file out before he locked the gates. Mikey stayed at the back to make sure no one got left behind.

The long cavalcade of pink pigs, all shapes and sizes, began to move slowly but steadily down the lane, led by a small but determined red pig with black spots.

22.

Spinning Pigs

Honky stayed at the front, focused and alert for anyone approaching. She could hear Mabel scolding and urging pigs to behave. It was still early Sunday morning, and there should be no one on the lane yet. But Honky wouldn't let herself breathe easily until they were down the lane and safely concealed under the trees by the stream. She was relieved when Hugo caught up with her.

'I'll trot on to the next bend and make sure no one's coming,' said Honky. She took off with impressive speed to a twisted beech tree in the hedgerow where she knew she would have a bird's eye view of the lane ahead.

That pig can move when she wants to, thought Hugo admiringly.

But Honky was panting by the time she reached the tree. Her breathlessness was understandable as pigs have no sweat glands and relatively small lungs for their size. She craned her neck to look down the lane to the cottage, and her fast-beating heart almost stopped. A woman was approaching with two Labrador dogs. Honky froze and shrank back behind the tree, almost forgetting to raise her trotter to alert the others.

Why is she out walking so early? Honky thought, panicked. *And of all the country lanes, why did she have to pick this one?*

Hugo saw the alert, and so did Mabel and Len and three hundred or so pigs tried to stuff themselves into the ditch and hedgerows around them. The sows and Len were too big to hide, so they shrank into the early morning shadows and hoped the danger would pass. Hugo stood near Len in the shadows.

'We may have to make a run for it,' Hugo whispered. His heart was thumping. He didn't know what danger lay ahead.

Honky's heart started to race again as the dogs got the pigs' scent. They leapt forward, straining at their leads, dragging the woman with all their strength. Honky's heart began to thump so loudly she was sure the woman could hear her. She squeezed back behind the tree, pressing herself into the hedge, praying the woman wouldn't let the dogs off their leads. The woman was struggling to contain the dogs. One of them was barking furiously now.

'Heel! Heel! Stop, stop, Goldie. Quiet down, Rufus! You'll wake the entire county.'

Still, she advanced, barely holding on to the two dogs. As the woman got closer and closer, Honky prayed fervently to the pig gods.

Please, please, turn around. Please turn around and go away...

It seemed the pig gods were listening.

'Right, I've had enough of you two,' the woman said, scolding the straining, growling and barking dogs. She turned around and strode off in the opposite direction dragging the dogs behind her. The looked over their shoulders, straining desperately to get off their leashes as she pulled them down the lane.

Honky breathed a massive sigh of relief. As soon as the woman and her dogs faded out of sight, she beckoned the others. They all emerged from the hedgerows.

'I heard the dogs,' said Hugo, catching up with Honky.

'A woman was walking them. Thank goodness, they turned around.'

'Hurry!' said Hugo beckoning all the pigs with urgency. 'We have to move fast now before anyone else comes.'

They reached the rusty old cottage gate, and Hugo swung it open while Honky led everyone past the cottage and behind the barn. Hugo's eyes were peeled on the lane ahead, and his ears were trained on the lane behind. His heart was racing, and his mouth was dry. He thought he would never herd the pigs through the gate quick enough. When the last pig and Mikey passed through, Hugo closed the gate and put the dummy chain around it again to look like it was padlocked. Only then could he breathe normally again. The pigs were already tucking into the summer grass, and the piglets were dancing around under their mothers' feet. Len was busy ordering the pigs to all move on and not linger around at the gate where they were visible from the lane.

'Listen up now. There will be plenty of time for eating grass when we get to where we are going. We've got to keep moving now. Follow Honky,' he barked.

Hugo turned to Mikey and gave him a giant hug of relief.

'We're not home and dry yet, but we're getting there.'

The cortege wasn't as tense now. Honky relaxed once everyone made it through the gates, and her ease transmitted back along the line. Mabel walked up to the front with Honky now, chatting quietly.

'I dreamt about this day,' said Mabel, gazing around her in wonder at trees and grass and hedgerows. She looked up to see blue skies for the first time in her life.

'I can't believe it has come about.'

Honky's heart soared, and she couldn't resist doing one of her happy spins, and seeing her, Mabel and hundreds of the other pigs started spinning too.

23.

A Dream Come True

Mabel craned her neck to see beyond the hedges of the cottage garden.

'How much further do we have to go to get the stream?' she asked.

'We go through that gap in the hedge there, into the field and down the hill,' said Honky, nodding in the direction of the stream. 'I think you are all going to love it there.'

When the pigs reached the barn, Mabel and Len pushed them behind it, out of sight of anyone who might come in the gate.

Hugo desperately hoped today wouldn't be the day that Farmer Herbert would want to visit the barn. The plan seemed perfect on paper. When Farmer Herbert was collecting his cows for milking on the far side of the stream, the pigs would be hidden behind the shed. At any other time, if Farmer Herbert came to the barn, the pigs should be concealed down among the trees by the stream.

Hugo pulled a penknife out of his rucksack and opened a straw bale in the barn. He started to tug the straw out and carry bundles of it in his arms around the back of the barn. The arrival of the straw was the signal for much hilarity and high jinks as the pigs discovered how much fun straw was. First, they tossed it up in the air and then threw themselves into piles of it, rolling and wriggling in delight. Then they got up and charged about snorting hysterically.

Hugo would have preferred if they made less noise and were less conspicuous. But he tried to relax. *They need to let off steam,* he thought. *They've been tense and uptight for a long time. And I know how that feels.*

So, he stood watching them, smiling and looked over at Honky, who smiled back at him.

'Mabel knows what straw is now!'

'I doooooo, and it's wonderful,' Mabel squealed, forgetting herself. 'It's squeeeeeeeeee! It's funneeeee!'

After a while, the pigs began to calm down and enjoy their new world. Some of them began rooting; others continued playing in the straw. The sows lay down on their sides, revelling in the vast space they had, as they called their piglets for food. Hugo watched as the sows talked to their piglets, giving regular rhythmic grunts as they fed. He saw the piglets line up at the correct teat, established as their own from the day they were born.

From his position behind a rhododendron bush, Mikey spied on Farmer Herbert as he collected his cows in the meadow on the far side of the stream. Later, Mikey watched as the farmer returned the cattle after milking. His giant radar ears heard the farmer's quad bike disappear, so he returned to the barn.

'It's all clear to go to the stream,' he announced.

The pigs were even more excited now. They were going to their new home.

'Okay, Honky, lead the way,' said Hugo. 'Mabel and Len, can you ask everyone to carry some of the straw with them?'

Hugo dragged a big bag of feed from the pallet in the barn, and with a lot of huffing and puffing, flung it onto Mikey's back and the odd caravan of three hundred pigs, a donkey and a boy started streaming down the hill.

The pigs gasped in joy and awe at their new home under the shady trees. Mabel had tears in her eyes as she saw the piglets squeal with delight at the crystal-clear running water. She looked around at the lush grass surroundings.

'This is a dream come true,' she breathed, mesmerised by the fresh air and the sky and the green around her. 'But even in my dreams, I never saw anything so beautiful.'

Len looked dazed and distracted, gazing around in wonderment too, as Hugo tried to explain that one bag of feed had to last a day.

'There's plenty of grass in the field to supplement the feed,' explained Hugo. 'Len? Len? Are you listening to me?'

Hugo saw that Len had to shake himself to focus.

'As soon as it gets close to milking time, you'll see the cows move up the field to the gates. That's your cue to make sure that the pigs race up the hill and hide behind the shed. Mikey will let you know when the cattle are back in the field, and the farmer is gone. You'll have to make sure Farmer Herbert doesn't see you coming up or down the hill, so leave the stream plenty of time before milking and make sure Mikey lets you know the coast is clear before you come back down here.'

He added: 'Honky and I will be back this evening. Can you keep everything together until then?'

Len nodded.

'No problem at all.'

Being the tallest and having the biggest and best ears, Mikey agreed to be the lookout. So, knowing the pigs were in safe hands, Honky and Hugo rushed back to their respective homes and crept into their beds before anyone noticed they were missing.

24.

Nerves

Honky was so exhausted that she slept soundly. She didn't even stir when Annie approached the woodshed with concern. It wasn't like Honky to miss her feed, and yet she hadn't appeared this morning.

'Honky, are you not having breakfast?' said Annie peering into the woodshed.

Honky stretched and yawned, and Annie sighed with relief.

'Oh, you're just a little lazybones this morning, aren't you?'

Hugo also slept but was woken by the sound of a big tractor outside his window. He looked out and scowled as he saw Farmer Farrelly cutting the long grass. *Sugar!* he thought. *Mikey won't have much grass now.* He heard strains of classical music coming from his parent's bedroom. They were still in bed, reading the papers and listening to the radio.

That day moved at a snail's pace for both friends. Honky felt anxious and went into Farmer Herbert's fields to stare up at the old cottage on the hill, but it was too far away to see anything. So, she went to lie in the shade near the yew tree and wait for Hugo instead. She was dozing when the dogs disrupted her peace.

Why are those dogs always barking like lunatics? she wondered grumpily.

But Honky was too curious to ignore a commotion, so she followed the dogs as they ran to the gate. A big jeep had pulled up outside. She reached the gate as the car door opened, and James jumped out.

Honky shrank back. *Not him!* she thought. *What's he doing here? Does he know the pigs are gone already?*

James had no trouble opening the gate, and he strode up to the front door and knocked. Honky's heart sank, and she started to shake with fear. *Does he know about Hugo and me?*

She watched as Annie answered the door.

'Come in for a minute. I'm not ready.'

They disappeared inside and closed the door. Honky hung around nervously but couldn't hear anything. Then, after what seemed like an age, the door opened again, and she could hear Annie chatting.

'The market is owned and run by a big cheese crowd, but they have other food stalls there and fabulous cakes and coffee. I thought it might be nice to go over because they have a jazz band on a Sunday as well.'

'Sounds great. I'm looking forward to it,' said James, opening the passenger door of his car for Annie.

Honky exhaled again. So, no one was talking about 300 missing pigs. Still, she couldn't decide which was worse – James discovering all his pigs had vanished or that he and Annie were becoming friends.

Honky wandered back to her shady spot and lay down. *This day is never going to end,* she thought. But time marched on regardless, and soon it was coming up to teatime for the pigs. Annie still wasn't back, and Honky started to panic again. It would soon be time to leave with Hugo and head back to the pigs.

What if she's not back before I have to leave, she wondered. *If I'm not here for my tea, Annie is going to search for me.*

Honky needn't have worried. At five o'clock on the dot, she heard a car slowing down out on the road and reversing into the drive. Annie jumped out and waved to the driver.

'Bye-bye! Talk soon!'

Annie had fed the animals and returned to the house by the time Honky heard Hugo's trademark pallet rattle.

'Let's go, Honky. Today seemed like the longest day of my life.'

'Me too, Hugo. Farmer James was here, you know.'

'No!' said Hugo, his eyes wide with shock.

'He called for Annie. That automatic feeder must be on all today because he doesn't know his pigs are gone.'

Hugo exhaled.

'Excellent. That gives us more time to get organised.'

When they reached the lane, they walked quickly to the cottage gate. Honky ran through the bars, and Hugo climbed over. There was no sign of life, nothing to give the game away. Hugo gave a huge sigh of relief.

'I half expected to see a load of pigs lolling around visible from the road.'

'Not with Mikey on the job,' replied Honky. 'Poor Mikey has a lot to lose if this goes horribly wrong. He'll be seen, and someone will take him away.'

The barn was empty and cool, and there was no sign of any pigs. They could see the cows were back in the meadow after the evening milking, so the two friends headed down to the stream. It was a warm evening, and the pigs were all making the most of their newfound freedom. Some were lying stretched out under shady trees or out in the cool grass. Others were in the stream, wallowing and splashing about. Mikey was there too, with a grin that reached from ear to ear.

'This is the most fun I've had in years! I've never had so much company or been surrounded by so much happiness!'

'So, it's all been good since we left?' asked Hugo.

'Totally,' he answered. 'They've all been doing what Len and Mabel tell them to do, and I am moving about, keeping an eye out.'

Mabel appeared from the trees at that moment. Her eyes were bright and her spirits high.

'I think I have died and gone to heaven. We're living like the ancient boars, like our ancestors. If I die now, I will die happy. All time I was telling the others stories about freedom, I wondered if I would ever experience it.'

'I'm so happy for you Mabel,' Honky said.

'Me too' said Hugo.

'Me three' said Mikey, and he started to curl his lip to hee-haw.

'Nooooooo!' they all shouted in unison. 'No hee-hawing! We can't attract any attention here!'

'Oops, I forgot! Sorry about that,' said Mikey with a big sheepish grin.

25.

No News is Good News

Mabel joined Hugo and Honky as they sat in the shade of an old elm tree by the stream. Hugo peeled off his socks and shoes and stretched his long legs. He picked a blade of grass and started to chew it.

'Do you like grass too?' asked Mabel, her head cocked to one side in curiosity.

'No, humans can't digest grass, but chewing on something helps me think.'

Hugo saw Mikey wander down to the stream for a drink, and he could see Len lying by the stream, basking in the warm evening rays of the sun. The piglets tumbled and ran around their dozing mothers. It was a blissful and restful scene, but how long could it last?

Hugo had only thought this far forward and no more. Even if no one discovered them, the food would run out within weeks. Then, the weather would change, and the pigs would need permanent shelter. He closed his eyes and considered what would happen when James discovered his entire pig herd had vanished. With a start, he wondered if the disappearance of 300 pigs would make the news. He was thankful that his parents rarely watched television, not even the news.

When they had moved here first, they didn't even own a television. Then his parents hired Molly, and she threatened to quit when she discovered there wasn't a television in the house, so they hurriedly bought one. Hugo watched nature documentaries mainly, but tonight he wanted to watch the news.

As the evening stretched on, Hugo realised he had to get back before his parents missed him. *I don't want them to start quizzing me and start watching where I'm going now,* he thought.

He saw Honky yawning and realised if he didn't move her now, he'd never get her home. After pulling on his socks and shoes, he told Mikey, grazing at the stream, that he and Honky were leaving.

'Remember to move everyone again before Farmer Herbert comes to start the milking in the morning.'

'I'm always awake at cockcrow,' Mikey assured him.

Honky and Hugo left with Mikey's fond eyes watching them as they made their way home quickly down the lane and through the fields.

When Hugo returned home, he found his parents sitting in the garden reading in the evening sun. He told them he was going in to watch television.

'That's nice, pet,' said his dad, but neither he nor his wife looked up from their books. Hugo dashed to the TV room, frantically flicking through all the channels for news. He only found soaps and game shows. He settled himself on the couch, prepared to wait for as long as necessary. Finally, the nine o'clock news came on RTE at half-past nine. Hugo shook his head in annoyance. He liked order, structure and logic.

'How can it be the nine o'clock news if it's not on at nine o'clock?' he grumbled.

Hugo listened to a series of mind-numbing reports about politics. There was nothing about escaped pigs or stolen pigs or even missing pigs. He was about to turn the TV off when his father came in from the garden.

'Hugo, bedtime. It's getting late.'

He said good night to his parents and fell into bed after setting his alarm carefully for 5.00am.

Back on Annie's farm, Honky returned to find the dogs were in the house and the other pigs were snoring quietly in their beds. No one had noticed she was missing. She slumped exhausted into her bed in the woodshed. It had been a long and stressful day. She didn't even bother to ruffle up and shake her straw.

Just before she closed her eyes, she whispered a little prayer to the pig gods.

'Please let them have a few days of freedom before they are found.'

With that, she fell fast asleep, dreaming about being chased by men with sticks. It made for a night of very restless and uncomfortable sleep, and her legs moved as if she was running as fast as she could.

26.

The Discovery

The machinery rumbled and shuddered, but the noise was muted by the ear-protecting earmuffs that James wore. He had started working a night shift at the factory that would continue until first thing in the morning. He didn't even hear Billy, the maintenance man, approaching from behind on his fork truck. Billy had to dismount and tap James on the shoulder to hand him the slip of paper. The scribbled message read: Call - urgent! (095) 231 99071

He recognised it as the number for Charlie, the farm manager. He removed his earmuffs and went over to Peter on the line.

'Problem on the farm - got to make a call,' he yelled over the sound of the machinery.

Peter nodded.

James went to his locker for his mobile phone. He had to walk outside the plant to get coverage, and that meant going out past security. He dialled the number as he was walking.

Charlie answered immediately.

'James, I'm here to check the pigs - and they're gone.'

'Gone? What do you mean *gone*? How can they be gone?'

'I mean every pen is empty. There's not a pig left in here.'

Charlie explained he was met by a deafening silence when he entered the shed. He said he stood there stunned for half a minute. The roller doors were closed; the main gates as well. It didn't make any sense. He ran around the farm to check, but there was no sign of any pigs anywhere.

'I still can't figure out where they are or even how they got out.'

'I'll be there as quick as I can. I have to sort out someone to cover for me here.'

Charlie assured him he would stay put.

James made a call to one of the other line managers and told him what had happened. The line manager agreed to cover the rest of James's shift. He knew James would return the favour to him when he needed it.

James jumped into his jeep and was back at the farm in 20 minutes. He still didn't believe it. It sounded like some outlandish joke. He ran past Charlie straight to the shed and looked in the open roller doors. Nothing. Not a pig to be seen. His mind was racing, but he couldn't make any sense of it. *How could 300 pigs vanish into thin air?* He shook his head in disbelief as he stared around at the empty pens.

'I better ring the guards.'

James rang the main station in Boarswood, a big station that was open all night. The garda on the end of the line sounded sceptical.

'Gone? 300 pigs gone? Have you checked the entire farm?'

James found it hard to believe himself even though he was looking into the empty shed. The garda said they would send a car right over. He sat with Charlie in the jeep, trying to figure out what had happened.

'This is absolutely mad. I can't get my head around it. How could they have got enough lorries in here to clear out all those pigs without anyone seeing?

James could see Charlie was as bewildered as he was.

A squad car swung in the gates, and two gardaí got out.

'I appear to have had my entire pig herd stolen,' said James.

The two guards poked their heads into the shed as if to make sure. Then the more senior one took out his notebook.

'We'll need a statement, so.'

He quizzed James and Charlie about the times they had last been in the yard and when they had last seen the pigs. Then he asked them to show him inside the shed to see how the pens and doors opened. They spent about half an hour looking around, and they walked the fields of James' farm, asking questions.

'I'm going to have to put out an all stations alert on this one,' said the senior guard. 'My super will probably want to alert the media and local marts first thing in the morning.'

James shook his head in disbelief again.

'Don't worry. We'll figure out what happened to them, and in the meantime, we will make those pigs way too hot to handle.'

James and Charlie were left looking into the dark empty cavern of the shed after the guards drove off.

'There's not much we can do here,' said James. 'You're as well to go home, and I'll give you a call in the morning if I've any news.'

James decided he may as well go back to work. He wouldn't have been able to sleep anyway with this disaster running through his head. Back at the factory, he relieved Michael, who had come in to cover for him and told him what had happened. Michael shook his head in disbelief. He was a dairy farmer, and he knew what he would feel if his whole herd went missing. He put a meaty hand on James' shoulders.

'Don't worry. The guards will find them,' he said.

James spent the rest of his shift wondering what could have happened to his pigs, so his mind was barely on the job. Soon, word spread around the factory, and all the workers, most of whom were other small farmers, came and offered their support.

His shift dragged on, but finally, the morning dawned, and he checked his mobile phone. Nothing. He walked to his jeep dejectedly. He had a quick shower before the guards called. They were sending out a senior investigator, so he went back down to the farmyard and sat in his jeep, listening to local radio as he waited.

We interrupt this programme to bring you an important message, the announcer said. Up to 300 pigs have been stolen in a daring raid on a farm near Boarswood...

His phone rang half a minute later. It was Annie, and the shock in her voice was clear.

'I've just heard the news on the radio. What happened?'

James told her as much as he knew, and she listened in stunned silence.

'Is there anything I can do?'

'Not really. I'll give you a call later when I know more.'

His phone rang again immediately, and it never stopped ringing all day. Friends, family, neighbours, the media, the mart owners, local farmers and the gardaí were astounded by the story of the missing pigs.

27.

Meltdown

Honky and Hugo were at Farmer Herbert's farm from first light, and Mikey carried another bag of feed to the stream. The pigs were grunting and rooting happily, and Len was on patrol, trying to keep the younger ones from straying too far from the trees.

Farmer Herbert would soon collect his cows for milking, and the pigs would have to be ushered up the field and hidden around the back of the shed. It was Monday morning, and Hugo had school, so once he was reassured that everything was well, he set off for home with Honky accompanying him. By the time Annie heard the news about James' pigs and came out to check her own livestock, Honky was back and tucked up in her bed in the woodshed.

At half-past three that afternoon, the school bus dropped Hugo at his front gate. He saw Molly curled up on the couch watching TV, and he sprinted up the stairs, taking two steps at a time to his parent's bedroom. He turned on their radio and looked at his watch. He didn't have to wait long until the four o'clock news came on. Top of the news bulletin was a report about an entire herd of pigs being stolen in a daring raid in Boarswood.

...if you have any information about the missing pigs, please contact Boarswood Garda Station on 049 9000 9000...

His heart banged hard in his chest.

This is it, he thought. *We knew it wouldn't be long before they were discovered missing. So, what do we do now?*

Hugo was out of ideas. All he could do was run down the field and talk to Honky.

'The pigs have made the news,' he told Honky. 'I just heard it on the radio. Everyone's looking for them now.

'What are we going to do?' asked Honky. 'Should we move them somewhere else?'

'No,' said Hugo. 'We'll stay where we are. Sometimes the most unlikely place to look is right under your nose. That makes the stream the safest place.'

'I guess that kind of makes sense.'

'For now, they've got to keep out of sight.'

But Hugo sounded a lot braver than he felt. Now that the news had broken and the hunt for the pigs had started, he felt cornered. He didn't know what to do next. That evening, RTE screened a report about the stolen pigs. The abattoirs, the butchers, the marts and other pig farmers had been notified, and the herd number came up on the screen. It was the same number printed on the tags in the pigs' ears. The programme speculated on the number of lorries needed to transport all those pigs and the amount of time the heist must have taken.

'Somebody out there must have information,' intoned one of the gardaí in the investigation. Even Hugo's father looked up from his newspaper to watch the big news story of the area.

'Funny old world,' he muttered. 'Imagine stealing 300 pigs.'

If he only knew his son was the one behind "the heist", Hugo thought. He shivered as he considered what might happen to him. Would he go to jail? What would become of the pigs when they were discovered? How would they return to cold concrete pens and never eat grass, bury their noses in straw or root in damp mud again? Why was the world such an unkind place?

Hugo sat thinking about the terrible things that could happen and soon became extremely anxious and agitated. He started to hyperventilate, and as he did, he rocked backwards and forwards, moaning loudly. Hugo hadn't had a meltdown like this in a long time. His parents thought he had grown out of having them, but he couldn't help himself.

His father was by his side in an instant.

'Take a deep breath and hold it while I count to ten,' his father instructed. He crouched in front of Hugo and held his hands, stroking them in a gentle and soothing manner. Slowly Hugo's breathing started to become more even. Finally, the terrible trembling stopped, and he slumped back against the couch, exhausted.

His father spoke calmly to him.

'Now, what's the matter, Hugo? You've been so happy for weeks now. Tell me what the matter is, and I'm sure I can help.'

Hugo couldn't tell him. He couldn't talk to anyone apart from the animals. Humans, even his parents, didn't understand him, and his mother and father would be horrified if they learnt that he had stolen a man's pigs.

Annie was watching the same RTE report. She hadn't heard anything from James, but she figured he would ring her when he wanted to talk. Everyone in the village was talking about the heist. When she had been down in the agri stores earlier, it was all anyone was talking about. The stolen pigs were on everyone's minds, and they all discussed beefing up security on their farms. Nothing had ever happened like this before. It was a small close-knit community where everyone knew everyone, and neighbours always helped each other. She knew that everyone would be ringing James and offering help. *He's probably sick to death talking about it,* she thought.

At that moment, the dogs started barking. Annie opened the door to call them in and saw James' jeep pulled into the gate.

'Any news?'

'No. No one seems to know anything.'

'There's another film crew coming in the morning to make a report.'

'That's great. Hopefully, there will be some news soon,' said Annie as she boiled the kettle.

James stayed for an hour before he said good night. He didn't know what to do with himself the last few days. He could think of nothing but his missing pigs.

28.

The Media Circus

Hugo's meltdown was over. He felt overwhelmed by his thoughts earlier, but now he was much calmer and able to think clearly. He vowed that he would help keep the pigs free as long as he could, and he would ensure they enjoyed every moment of their freedom. He would find them food and shelter and care for them as best he could, and the pigs would enjoy the grass and the trees and the running spring water.

He could do nothing more. He reasoned he was only a boy, and he had no money or power. When the pigs were found, and it was inevitable that they would be, James would incarcerate them in that horrible concrete shed again. Their wonderful memories would be the only joy the pigs had then. Hugo had to hope that would be enough to sustain them. As for him, he would have to face the music, but he just wouldn't think about it now.

Early the next morning, Hugo and Honky relaxed at the stream with Mikey, Mabel and Len. The rest of the pigs were chuntering away together companionably.

'I don't ever want to be on my own here again,' said Mikey.

'And we never want to leave,' said Mabel.

'I'm really hoping that everyone can stay,' said Hugo.

'So, you have a plan?' Mikey asked, his eyes widening, his long ears flicking backwards. 'What's going to happen when we're found?'

'Honky thinks that Annie might be able to convince people to let you stay.'

Honky nodded furiously.

'I've heard her say a lot that pigs shouldn't be reared in concrete sheds.'

Hugo tried to reassure Mikey.

'I'm not worried about you, Mikey. I know we will be able to convince either my dad or Annie to give you a home.'

'I would be much happier to know we all could stay here,' replied Mikey, sadly.

I would too, thought Hugo.

Soon Hugo had to leave for school.

'I'm getting my summer holidays at the end of this week so I'll be able to come up every day for longer.'

'I'm going to stay longer today, Hugo,' said Honky. 'Annie is gone to work already. She fed us very early this morning.'

'Okay, I'll see you all this evening. Please be careful not to be seen.'

The school day dragged even more than usual for Hugo. His teacher even talked about the missing pigs. A nephew of James was a pupil in the class above him. In the schoolyard, he overheard him telling the older boys about the film crew coming to film at his uncle's farm. He boasted that they would want to talk to him as well.

'Will it be on the news tonight?' they asked.

'It's going to be on the news here and all over the world,' he replied importantly.

Hugo felt ill and couldn't listen to anymore, so he went out behind the shelter and sat on the ground on his own.

Meanwhile, James' farm was abuzz with activity as the latest camera crew descended. Their cars were parked all over the yard as they did sound checks and brandished big long metal poles with fluffy heads on them. James wasn't in the mood for this circus, but he knew it had to be done. The more people who knew about his stolen pigs, the more likely he would get them back.

But he was growing increasingly depressed since he got that phone call on Sunday night. He felt guilty about the pigs. What if they weren't being fed or were being badly treated? He was also very concerned about the enormous financial loss as he wasn't insured for theft on this scale. Now he effectively had no income from the farm but still had all the expenses associated with it. The feed companies had to be paid for feed delivered weeks ago. His helpers had to be paid - it wasn't their fault that they now had no work. He had electricity, diesel, county council rates and the haulage company that transported his pigs to the abattoir to pay. The list was endless. He was looking at the real possibility of being forced to sell the farm.

However, he knew selling would break his father's heart because the farm had been in their family for generations. The old man rang him several times a day asking for any news about the pigs. James tried to be up-beat, but it wasn't easy.

'So, can you tell us how you discovered your pigs had been stolen?'

James realised that he was on camera with a micro-phone thrust in his face and a reporter's steady gaze upon him.

The crew were with him for over an hour for a piece that would air for less than five minutes. But they were very kind to him and sympathetic. They could see how upset he was.

When they drove out the green gates, James turned to lock up and go home. However, as soon as he got into his jeep, he changed his mind and drove to Annie's.

29.

Crimecover

Annie got home from work early and started trying to repair some electric fencing that was shorting and making a constant clicking noise. She didn't even see James arriving until he reached her in the field. The dogs knew him by now and didn't bother barking anymore.

'Hey, how are you?' she said, surprised.

'I've been better, but look it could always be worse,' he said, attempting to sound more positive than he felt.

He told her about the film crew and the report that would be broadcast that night.

'You're welcome to watch it here with me because I will be glued to it,' she said.

He welcomed some company. It gave him something else to focus on rather than his missing herd of pigs and financial doom.

'That would be great,' he said. 'Do you need a hand with that?'

They sorted the electric fence, watered the pigs and went into the house. James confided his worries about losing the farm while Annie made tea.

'Gosh, I never thought it would come to that. Surely insurance will cover you?'

'The premium was going up and up every year, so I cut back on some cover. I don't have valuable machinery, so I figured I only needed the bare minimum for theft.'

He sighed heavily.

'I've been racking my brain all day thinking about how I could avoid selling the farm,' he said. He always said he was a reluctant farmer, but now that he faced losing his farm, he realised how much it meant to him.

'The stock, all those pigs, is going to be the biggest cost to replace,' he said. 'And even if I could afford to replace them, I'll have lost some valuable genetics. The pigs are descendants of pigs my father kept, so there's a sentimental link to the past too.'

'You know you have land too,' said Annie. 'Have you ever thought of changing your method of farming pigs?'

'What do you mean?'

'Restock slowly at a smaller density, and bring in some rare breeds that would thrive outdoors. That way, you would reduce your overheads, especially your feed bill. You also save on electricity and heat in the wintertime.'

She suggested selling directly to local butchers and farm shops to get a premium price for pork. She even advised on setting up a farm shop in his yard because some of the shed could be converted into a processing room to add value to his pork.

'Make your own sausages, puddings, that sort of thing.'

He sat pondering over her ideas.

'I know my father would be thrilled if I did that. Mainly because it would mean not having to sell the farm, but also because he is always complaining pork and bacon don't taste like they used to.'

The news came on, followed by the weather forecast, and finally, the theme tune to the programme, Crimecover, began.

'This is it,' said James, settling into the armchair beside the big open fireplace.

The reporter who had been on James' farm that day began the section by explaining that he would tell the viewers about a most unusual theft. First, the camera panned around James' farmyard and zoomed into the open door of his dark and silent pig shed. Then came the interview with James, and it was clear that he was upset about the theft.

The journalist concluded the report by saying: 'Of course, there will be a small reward for any information leading to the discovery of the missing pigs.'

Annie walked out to the gate with James afterwards. As he sat into the jeep, he took her hand and held it for an instant.

'I need to thank you for being such support to me,' he said.

'Really, James, it's nothing. What are friends for?'

Friends... friends, he thought as he drove down the road. I guess we are. He liked Annie. She was forthright and practical, and she had a good head on her shoulders. He needed all the friends he had now. He decided to call and see his father the next day and talk to him about all her ideas. The old man could do with some positive news.

30.

A Narrow Escape

Honky took off to see the fugitive pigs first thing every morning after being fed. Annie was working every day now, so she fed the pigs much earlier than normal. Stumpy was curious to know where Honky was always going in such a hurry.

'Where do you disappear to all the time?' she called as Honky passed their enclosure in the early morning again.

'I'm off to have a chat with my pal Hugo,' Honky said and hurried on her way.

The less she knows, the better, she thought.

Honky had to be doubly careful now that everyone was on the lookout for missing pigs and had to get down the lane early in the morning to avoid being spotted. She loved having pig friends like Mabel, and she enjoyed the fun with Mikey. She knew Hugo would soon finish school for the summer, and hopefully, they all could spend even more time together.

The pigs were all used to the routine now and disappeared out of sight during the milking hours. So far, no one had spotted them, and everyone felt relaxed. Honky arrived just in time to have a root around with Mabel, and then they had a wallow in the stream before lying down under a willow to talk. Mabel was fascinated by Honky's life.

'Did you really sleep in the house on the dog beds?' she asked.

'I did until Annie got fed up cleaning up my pee. But what did she expect when she locked me in? I did my best to get out, but I could never get the door open. I was delighted when she moved me outside to my own little house - the woodshed in the veg garden. It's so cosy and warm.'

'You are so lucky, Honky,' sighed Mabel.

'I guess I am, but you know I was very lonely until I met Hugo.'

'Tell me again about how you met him.'

Honky began the story, and Mabel sighed with contentment and stretched and yawned luxuriously. It was lovely to have stories told to her for a change.

Mikey stood at the top of the hill, watching all around him. He felt important and useful for the first time in ages, and it was a good feeling. Before Hugo filed his feet, Mikey couldn't move around much. He had been grazing on scrub, bracken, brambles and ivy around the cottage and had become thin and malnourished. Since Hugo had worked on his hooves, he grazed in Farmer Herbert's field and wherever he wanted. He was beginning to put on weight from the lush summer grass.

Just then, his ears twitched. Was it...? Yes, he definitely heard an engine approaching. He looked down the field and across the stream in the direction the sound came from. Someone was approaching on a tractor, but hopefully, they would drive straight past the field entrance. Len heard the tractor engine then too, and he and Mabel ushered everyone under the trees as a precaution.

But the tractor stopped at the gate, and suddenly, the vehicle rolled into the field. The tractor's arrival was not scheduled. Even the cattle stopped grazing and stared at the sudden and unexpected intrusion. Mikey could see their tails swishing in annoyance. *Is it Farmer Herbert?* he wondered. His heart was beating fast. He couldn't be sure from this distance, but he thought he could make out fencing poles and rolls of wire in the front loader. It looked like Farmer Herbert was about to put in some new fencing.

Down in the trees, the pigs stayed stock still and hardly dared to breathe.

'What should we do?' Mabel asked Len.

'We do nothing,' he said. 'We will just have to sit tight and see where he is going.'

The tractor went into the top corner of the field, and a man who wasn't Farmer Herbert got out. Mikey breathed a little easier. Farmer Herbert had the beady eye of a hunter and would spot the movement of any creature under the trees. Hopefully, this man would do his work and go.

Mikey watched as the man went over to the temporary electric fencing and began to pull the posts out, winding the electric wire around them. When he had taken all the fencing up, he got back into his tractor and tipped out the big heavy wooden posts and the rolls of wire. Then he drove out and back down the lane.

Mikey felt relieved. The man was gone for now, but he could be back at any stage by the looks of things, and they mightn't be so lucky the next time. Mikey wished Hugo would hurry up and return. Their safety depended on Farmer Herbert's strict schedule, and now these movements couldn't be relied upon anymore. Hugo might know what to do.

Shortly afterwards, Mikey and the pigs spotted Hugo approaching, and everyone rushed to tell him what had happened.

'Slow down, slow down,' said Hugo. 'One at a time, please.'

Mikey told him what happened, and Hugo gazed across the fields to where the man had dropped the fencing stuff.

'He must be a fencing contractor working for Farmer Herbert. It looks as if he's working up at that corner of the meadow now. Hopefully, he'll just return and do the fencing and stay away from the stream.'

'Hopefully....' they all muttered in unison, but they were shaken.

Mikey stood sentry at the stream this time. The pigs went back to spending the rest of the day the way they had become accustomed. The gloriously warm sunny days were perfect for wallowing down at the stream and then drying off under the spreading willow trees.

Hugo lay back against a gnarled tree trunk chewing a piece of straw and not for the first time worried about how much longer they could remain undiscovered.

31.

Spotted

They didn't have long to wait. First, the fencing contractor returned, but Mikey had been listening out for the earliest sound of his tractor. This time he alerted the pigs in time to move up the field and settle behind the barn safely out of sight.

The contractor spent a few hours fencing the temporary paddocks that Farmer Herbert used for mob grazing. Mob grazing involves corralling the cows into one fenced area for a short while and moving them on to another paddock after they eat all the grass. The farmer planned to rotate the cattle around the farm, giving the original paddocks a chance to recover and re-grow new grass.

The contractor set up gates between each paddock for the fluid and easy movement of the cattle. Hugo gazed at the design after he left and thought he had done a fantastic job. He loved anything to do with design and engineering, and the gates fascinated him.

Early next morning, Farmer Herbert arrived on schedule to collect his cows for milking. Mikey and the pigs waited and waited, but this time he didn't bring the cows back.

'I guess he has other land around his farmhouse, which can also be used for grazing,' said Mikey. 'I don't think the cows are coming back for a while.'

Mikey was uneasy with another change in the farmer's routine, but everyone returned to the stream when they realised the cows were not coming back. There was a lot of activity down at the stream that afternoon. The pigs splashed about in the water, and Mikey had his ears trained to the fields in front in case Farmer Herbert or the contractor returned. So, no one heard the quad bike purring up towards the cottage way behind them.

Farmer Herbert parked in the front of the barn and went in for some feed. It took a few minutes for his eyes to adjust to the darkness. But when he saw the straw pulled out from his tight bales, he was puzzled. He walked around scratching his head. Then he spotted the by now half-empty pallet of cow nuts with its torn plastic wrapping. He walked over to it and stood looking at it in disbelief.

He stomped around the cottage garden in a fury, looking for any evidence of thieves. He spotted the gap in the hedge leading to his fields and looked down to the stream. What he saw totally stunned him. It was like a scene on a Lanzarote beach, except all the sun worshippers were pigs. He saw pigs stretched in the sun, pigs wallowing, pigs snoozing in the shade and pigs splashing in the water watched over by a donkey 'lifeguard.' He stood with his mouth gaping open, taking a few minutes to process what he was seeing. He patted his jacket and realised he didn't have his phone with him. He wanted to ring James to let him know that he'd found his herd of pigs. Farmer Herbert looked again to make sure he was seeing correctly and then left, shaking his head in disbelief.

He got back to the farmyard, grabbed his phone from his jeep and rang James.

'You're not winding me up, are you, Alex?' James said.

'I swear I'm not. I couldn't believe my eyes. And the donkey who was at the cottage is in the middle of them.'

'Donkey?'

'Yes, I've been renting the barn at the cottage for extra storage, and a donkey appeared there months ago. I assumed the owners knew about it, and I didn't question it.'

'Yes, I think I've seen him, but how the heck did the pigs get out in the first place and find their way there? And who has been feeding and looking after them?' James said, more to himself than to Farmer Herbert.

'I don't know who has been feeding them,' said the other farmer. 'But they've gone through half a pallet of cattle nuts, and they're lying on a lot of the straw I had stored in the shed.'

'Don't worry about that, Alex. You know I'll reimburse you and pay for any damage. Is there much damage to the field?'

'Not a lot. The hot weather has meant the ground is too dry and hard for them to have done much rooting. They seem to have stayed near the trees all the time. It's like they knew to hide there. Most of the rooting has been confined to the area at the stream, and that will recover by itself.'

'I can't tell you how relieved I am that you've found them. I'm at work, but I'll call down to you as soon as I finish here. First, I better ring the guards and let them know they can call off the search.'

Farmer Herbert put the phone back down, and he was still shaking his head in wonderment as he went in to tell his wife.

James left the noisy factory floor to make a few phone calls, feeling equally stunned and relieved. His pigs were found, and he could save his farm.

He finished his shift and drove up to Farmer Herbert's. He called into Annie on the way to tell her. She stood looking at him with her mouth open in shock and disbelief.

'How could they have been right under you and Farmer Herbert's nose all this time, and no one realised?'

James shrugged in bewilderment.

'I don't know who was more surprised - Farmer Herbert or me. We still don't know what has been going on. Someone is feeding the pigs because half a pallet of nuts and his straw is missing from the barn.'

'What are you going to do now?' she asked.

'I've rung the guards, and they are letting the marts and everywhere else know. I will gather a crew together to herd the pigs back. Alex says they are okay where they are for now.'

'Alex is all right,' she said. 'He's a decent skin behind it all.'

'I'm heading down to the field now to see for myself. I'm going to call for Alex first, and I'll give you a ring later.'

Annie went back into the house, relieved that they found James' pigs. Farmer Herbert described seeing the pigs enjoying themselves as if they were at a beach resort. It would be hard on them to go back into their concrete confinement now, and she felt deeply sorry for them. She hated the way modern pigs were kept.

It's not natural to restrict pigs' normal behaviours and leave them bored out of their minds, she thought. She wished people would realise that it was not good for pork consumers either. The meat produced in this way was not as healthy because the pigs hadn't a natural grass and forage diet. Also, once confined in close quarters, the herd required antibiotics to avoid disease or illness spreading like wildfire.

For Annie, though, it was a welfare issue. She thought of her pet Honky. She was such a little character that she could never bring herself to take her to the abattoir. She found it heart-breaking to take any of her animals to slaughter, but that was the way of farming. However, she believed farmers should give every animal a chance to live its best life before then.

'No animal should live an unnatural life so we can eat,' she muttered out loud to no one in particular, and she slammed a cupboard door shut for emphasis.

32.

Discovered

Honky, Hugo and Mikey had no idea they'd been discovered. No one heard Farmer Herbert arrive at the barn, and no one had spotted him surveying the idyllic scenes at the stream. They were blissfully unaware that their dream was about to end. Mikey heard the engines first and pricked his ears. Then the others heard the convoy of cars approaching through the lane at the front of the cottage. Hugo scrambled up from the ground and stood beside Mikey. He knew they were coming for them.

'Sugar, we're really in for it now!' he whispered

'Take cover, everyone,' ordered Len, and all the pigs darted under the trees to try and hide.

'What will we do?' said Mikey.

'Nothing we can do,' said Hugo, his heart sinking into his boots.

Hugo shrunk back against a tree trunk and put his head into Mikey's neck. He started to shiver uncontrollably. Honky nuzzled his leg with her mucky snout.

'Don't worry, Hugo,' she said. 'Maybe they're not here for us.'

Hugo didn't answer because he wasn't able.

They heard the car engines stop at the cottage and the sound of multiple doors slamming closed. The guards,

Farmer Herbert and James strode down the field towards the stream. For the second time that day, Farmer Herbert was lost for words as he peered into the copse of trees. There was a boy in there too. A boy, a donkey and 300 pairs of pigs' eyes stared back at him. James stood staring dumbstruck at the sight under the trees as well.

Mabel spotted James and realised they had been discovered.

'Wuh-wuh, wuh-wuh, wuuuuuuuh,' she cried as she ran through the trees, rallying the pigs.

The pigs erupted, standing with nostrils flared, ready to stampede and flee. Honky marched out of the trees first and addressed the pigs.

'It's okay, stay where you are,' said Honky. 'We knew this day would come, and there is nothing we can do about it. It's in the hands of the pig gods now.'

They all listened to her and turned to watch the men. What was going to happen now?

James was still staring in astonishment at the only pig to appear from the trees. Unlike his pink pigs, she was a distinctive red, and she had a white face and black spots. There was no mistaking who she was.

'I know this pig!' he said to the others. 'She's not mine. She's a pet pig belong to Annie.'

What is going on? he thought. For an instant, he thought of Annie's passion for free-range farming and wondered if she had anything to do with this. But he remembered her shock and confusion over the disappearance of the pigs and dismissed the idea.

He barked at the boy in the trees.

'Who are you? Are you the mastermind behind this whole thing?' he asked.

Hugo's neck and face turned bright red, and he began to stammer nervously. James scratched his head and looked at the other men. They hadn't a clue what the boy was saying either, but it was clear he was terrified. James whipped out his phone and rang Annie.

'You better get over here now,' he said.

The stand-off continued as men continued to stare at the motley crew under the trees, and the pigs and the boy and the donkey stared back. Then, finally, they heard Annie's jeep came up the lane, and minutes later, she arrived to survey the same scene. She saw Honky and looked at her in complete disbelief.

'Honky? What on earth are you doing here? What's going on?'

Then she saw Hugo.

'Who are you?' she asked. Hugo stammered his name and tried to tell them that he lived near Annie.

Annie turned to James.

'Who is the child, and what on earth is going on?'

'We thought you might know...'

'How on earth would I?' she replied sharply.

James looked sheepish.

'One thing I do know is that this young man needs to be taken home, wherever that is,' he said.

Annie approached the trees and extended her hand to Hugo.

'Come on,' she coaxed. 'We're going to talk to your parents.'

Hugo emerged reluctantly, his cheeks flushed, and his head bowed.

Annie added: 'Honky get straight back home the way you came, or there will be trouble.'

Honky sighed and started her long journey home alone.

Once Anne was alone in the car with the boy, he relaxed, and she could understand his name and where he lived.

He only lives down the road! How come I don't know this child or his family? she wondered.

She parked outside the gates of Hugo's house and rang the intercom. She told the man who answered that she was his neighbour and had their son with her.

The gates opened slowly, and Hugo's father stood waiting at the open door.

'Hello, I'm Annie, and I think you better put the kettle on and sit down,' she said. 'This young man has a lot to tell you.'

33.

The Parents

Hugo's parents sat at the table in stunned silence. They were sure Annie had made a terrible mistake. How on earth could their quiet little boy have been behind the great big pig robbery?

'I think we better hear about it from the horse's mouth,' said Hugo's father. Hugo hung his head and had said nothing while Annie outlined what the farmers and the guards had discovered. Hugo sat at the table, occasionally shivering.

Annie was soft-spoken and kind.

'Hugo, can you tell us all about this, please? We need your help in understanding what this is all about.'

Hugo started to talk, got flustered and stopped.

'It's okay, Hugo,' said his father. 'Begin at the beginning, slowly.'

Hugo stopped shivering and started to tell the adults what he had done, hesitantly at first, but then when he realised they were all calm, he became less nervous. The mother and father could understand Hugo better than Annie, but she grasped the bones of the story.

They listened to how he had met Honky, made friends with her, discovered Mikey in the old cottage and how the pig farm troubled him. Hugo talked for ages, and they only interrupted to ask an occasional question or ask him to repeat himself. Hugo then slumped in his chair, ashen-faced and exhausted.

'Hugo has to go to bed,' said his mother. 'Hugo, pet, go on up. I'll be up in a little while to you,'

Hugo walked up the stairs to his bedroom slowly. His heart was heavy. He wasn't worried about what might happen to him, but he was fretting about the pigs and Mikey. He was exhausted, and when he lay down, he was fast asleep in seconds.

After Hugo went to bed, his dad put on the kettle again, and Annie suggested they ring James and tell him to come in. James was outlining a plan to move the pigs with Farmer Herbert when Annie called and asked James to join her at Hugo's house.

'This is something you need to hear,' she said.

James shook Hugo's parents' hands, accepted their apologies for their son's behaviour and sat down. The mother handed him a cup of tea and took down the biscuit tin.

Annie started to tell James all Hugo had told them as he sat in complete silence.

'I'm sorry if I sounded suspicious, Annie. When I saw your pig in the middle of it all, it crossed my mind that you were somehow involved.'

'Well, it's hard to believe that a small boy could have done all this with just the help of a pig and a donkey,' said Hugo's mother. 'But what's going to happen now? Will you press charges?'

James shook his head.

'Look, I have my pigs back, and they seem to be in good condition. So I don't think it would benefit anyone to get the law involved.'

Annie was curious about Hugo and his lack of verbal skills.

'Yes, Hugo is different to other kids,' said his mother. 'He's autistic.'

'But he's high functioning,' added his father.

'What does that mean?' asked Annie.

Hugo's father explained that although Hugo was autistic and had communication difficulties, he was highly intelligent.

'He seems to have a particular flair for engineering and design,' he said. 'His teachers have noticed it.'

'Well, he is obviously very smart to have pulled off the biggest pig heist ever in this country,' laughed Annie. 'How did you not notice he was missing for so much time?'

Hugo's parents admitted they were mortified that they hadn't noticed his lengthy disappearances. They explained they both worked an hour away at the university and left Hugo with his minder.

'Obviously, she hasn't been doing too much minding,' his mother said.

Hugo's father walked out to the gate as Annie and James left.

'It was lovely to meet you and talk,' he said. 'It's just a shame it's happened under these circumstances.'

Annie and James had a brief chat at their cars.

'When the media get a hold of this story, all hell is going to break loose,' she said.

'I don't know whether anyone will even believe it,' he replied.

Annie was tired and needed a good night's sleep, so she said she better get back to the farm. She was also still a bit hurt and annoyed that James suspected she had been involved too. The first thing she did when she reached home was check on Honky. She looked in at her, snuggled into a bed of straw, fast asleep and shook her head in wonderment. *Imagine, a bunch of adults being outsmarted by a pig and a kid!*

34.

A Wake-up Call

James returned to the old cottage on the edge of Farmer Herbert's land and stood at the top of the hill looking down at the stream. It was still warm, and most of the pigs lay stretched out below in the twilight. He watched them for ages, saw them roll and turn and stretch contentedly, and a sense of calm descended on him. It was so peaceful watching animals living the way nature intended. He wondered how he could farm this way rather than intensively.

It was all very well for Annie with a handful of pigs, but would it work with the number he had? There was a lot to think about because he would need to use the land he had leased. And the lease was almost up, so he had to make a quick decision. He didn't want to be unfair to Farmer Grimes, who leased it from him. He stayed there until the light faded, and he could only see the dark silhouettes of the trees at the stream.

It was late, but he called in to see his father nearby to tell him the news. He knew the old man would be up.

'The pigs were found, Dad,' he said.

The older man leant on his walking stick and beamed from ear to ear.

'My prayers have been answered,' he said before firing a million questions at James. They sat for a while and talked, and James broached the subject of changing from intensive to organic farming.

'I don't think we have enough land,' said his father.

'No, not unless I reduce the herd considerably or lease more. My friend Annie thinks that if I switch to rare breed pigs, it will provide big savings because they don't need to be in constant heat.'

'It makes sense,' his father agreed. 'There are breeds that are much better adapted to living outdoors and have a bigger fat layer and heavy winter coats.'

'The only thing that would worry me is the fat layer,' mused James. 'Annie says customers are so brainwashed that fat is bad she sometimes finds it hard to sell hers. So, she has started to 'cut the carbs' when feeding her pigs - the way many people do to lose weight.'

The old man rubbed his chin.

'She might be onto something there. Long ago, when we fed our pigs too many spuds, they got as fat as butter.'

Then he added: 'You know you could turn your pig business into a proper industry.'

'How so?' asked James.

The old man happened to repeat a lot of suggestions Annie had made. For example, James could get local growers to supply his grain and field beans for protein. He mentioned a local publican who had diversified into a micro-brewery and created a range of Baker Brew craft beers. He said James could make use of The Baker Brew's waste products like spent barley. And then there was the German lady making cheese who had by-products that were useful for pigs.

'She would have whey, and I'm sure would do a deal with you, if you offered her whey-fed pork in return.'

James and his father sat for ages talking about all the endless possibilities. For the first time in ages, he felt enthusiastic and optimistic about the future of the farm. He was fed up killing himself and barely managing to break even. It required a second income from the factory to keep him afloat. If it hadn't been for his father, the farm would have been long sold. What happened was a wake-up call. He knew he needed to change his life and the way he farmed.

'Maybe things happen for a reason,' his dad said.

'Maybe,' said James.

He thought about this as he drove home and about the media storm that would erupt when they discovered the pigs had been stolen by an autistic schoolboy and a black-spotted red pig. James sighed. He needed a decent night's sleep before his brain exploded.

35.

Viral

James was right about the media storm, but it was even bigger than he anticipated. With the help of social media, the story went viral and made headlines all around the world. His phone started ringing at dawn. James groaned, turned off the phone and rolled over.

Annie nearly dropped her mug of tea when she heard her name and Honky's mentioned on the radio in a news report about the pigs' discovery.

'How did they find out about Honky?' she gasped aloud. 'And that she belongs to me? Oh no, they're going to be all over us like a rash.'

Her phone started ringing, but she didn't recognise the number. *Reporters calling already?* she wondered. Would she have reporters at the gates soon? Or worse, reporters coming over the gates and spooking the pigs?

Better stay home until this dies down, she thought. She decided to ring her boss and ask for a few days off. When she told Jan Spice what happened, he immediately agreed that she should remain at home and told her to take a week off.

She rang James after she hung up from work.

'Did you get any sleep?'

'I did until my phone started hopping at first light, so I turned it off. I just switched it back on, and you rang.'

'I think it's going to be a crazy few days. I'm worried about Hugo and all this media attention. I better talk to Hugo's parents.

'And I'm going to see if I can track down the owners of that donkey.'

James phoned a few local farmers to see if anyone knew anything about Mikey's owner. It didn't take long to find out that the man died six months previously. The donkey didn't have an owner anymore, and James wondered if it might be possible to keep the animal. After all, he recalled reading that donkeys chase foxes out of their territory, and if he did start free-ranging his pigs, he would need a fox deterrent to prevent his newborn piglets from being taken.

James rang an official from the department of agriculture for advice, and the official recommended he ring the Donkey Sanctuary. James spoke to a helpful woman who assured him it was perfectly legal to keep Mikey. She suggested he read their website pages on donkey care, and if he had any questions, she would be happy to answer them.

Next James contacted his farmhands and scheduled to meet them the next day to help move the herd back to his farm.

As he pulled up to Annie's house later, two cars stopped behind him, and a man and two women jumped out and ran to his window.

'Have you any comment to make about your stolen pigs?'

'Can we see the pet pig who was involved?'

'Where does the young boy live – the one who was also involved?'

'No comment,' said James politely as he opened the gate and drove into Annie's.

She sighed as she looked at the people at the gate.

'They're coming here all morning. It's crazy. I spoke to Hugo's mother before she left for work and told her that the media want to interview Hugo. I said we wouldn't tell them where Hugo lived but that someone was bound to. She agreed that there is no way Hugo could handle all that.'

James knew the last thing they needed was a load of strangers crawling all over the locality and causing mayhem.

'Maybe if I issue a short statement and explain that Hugo couldn't handle the stress, they might leave him alone. We'll have to talk to his parents first, of course. I think I'll have to do an exclusive interview with one radio and television station, and that should bring an end to it.'

'Gosh, you are getting quite good at all this, aren't you?'

He laughed.

'I'm good at lots of things, especially losing pigs.'

36.

The Pig Gods are Listening

Honky heard the rattle of the pallet, and when she raced to the fence, Hugo was waiting for her.

Honky was delighted to see him.

'I have news,' she said. 'And I need to tell Mabel and the pigs. When can we see the others?'

'I don't know,' Hugo replied. 'I've been thinking about it all night, but they're watching me like a hawk now. I'll have to get back in a minute before they miss me. What's the news you have to share?'

'I was hanging around the patio door when Annie and James were talking, and I think the pigs are being moved back to James' farm tomorrow.'

Hugo's face fell. It was the worst news.

'But get this, they also said something about Mikey being useful if James decides to let the pigs become free-range pigs.'

'Free-range? Honky, you're not saying that to get my hopes up, are you? '

'I swear on my life, Hugo. I heard them saying it. Maybe Farmer James is not as bad as I thought.'

'That would be amazing if it was true. I'm worried sick about the pigs and Mikey.'

'I might try to get out after dark and let the others know.'

'Just be careful, Honky,' Hugo pleaded, and then he rushed home before his parents missed him.

At that time, the animals at Farmer Herbert's stream were subdued and sad. Both Farmer Herbert and Farmer James had come to feed them and had confined the pigs to a narrow area around the trees. The two erected electric fencing so they couldn't move outside this area.

Mikey stood on the other side of the electric fencing with his head drooping. He had spent hours talking to Mabel and Len, and all three were worried. They hadn't spoken to Hugo or Honky since they were discovered.

'I hope they're not in jail,' piped up Mabel.

'Don't be silly, Mabel. They don't put children or pigs in jail,' said Len.

The day dragged on slowly because they were all anxious and worried. They didn't know what had happened to their friends, Hugo and Honky, and they knew nothing about their fates either.

The pigs settled down for the evening. It was extremely mild, and they loved sleeping outdoors. However, Len and Mabel secretly worried about when this freedom would end.

The light had faded and everyone was sleeping when Honky appeared at the fence. The pigs scrambled to their feet in excitement. They gathered in front of her asking a hundred questions at once.

'Hang on, hang on. Let me catch my breath. I've been holding so much in all day waiting for my opportunity to sneak up here.'

Honky told them she had overheard plans for a free-range farm, and they all gasped in unison.

'Really, do you think that's true?' said Mikey with tears in his eyes.

'That's what they talked about. That's all I know.'

'Maybe the pig gods are listening to us, so,' Mabel said, and a new light shone in her eyes for the first time since the pigs were discovered.

'Just make sure to behave when they come to move you. We don't want James thinking that being free-range is more trouble than it's worth.'

Honky told them that Hugo's parents were watching him like a hawk, and he wasn't allowed out anymore. But Honky said Hugo missed them all.

'Tell him we've been missing him too,' said Mikey. 'And thank you for coming and bringing us hope.'

'Annie still hasn't spotted my escape routes, but she's watching me far more, and she's not going out these days, especially since all these strange people keep coming to the gate and shouting in at her.'

Honky had watched as Annie put a huge chain around the gate and put barbed wire on top. Still, all these people were sitting outside in cars, causing a traffic jam on the road outside. They were a nuisance. The pallet was near the gate, making it more difficult for her and Hugo to meet or escape without being seen.

Honky made for home and ran along the short stretch of road to reach the pallet. She could still see the line of car lights outside Annie's gate in the dark.

Who are those people? she wondered as she squeezed through the back of the pallet into Annie's farm.

'Honky!'

She leapt as someone hissed her name in the dark. It was Hugo.

'You scared the life out of me!'

'Sorry, I've been waiting ages for you. My parents think I'm asleep. How did you get on? Are the pigs okay?'

She told him they all missed him and said their hopes soared once she told them about the conversation she'd overheard.

'I just hope I heard right, Hugo.'

'I hope so too, Honky.'

37.

Whole New World

Annie and James gave an exclusive interview to RTE and told them the true story of the runaway pigs. They told them about the little boy who secretly made friends with Annie's free-range piglet, and when he saw intensively farmed pigs, he was so upset that he felt compelled to free them. So, with the piglet and a donkey, he led 300 pigs to a copse of trees by a local stream where they all hid out for days.

Instead of the media interest waning, however, it became a feeding frenzy. The report was picked up and broadcast by news stations all over the world. TV stations and media across America, Australia, New Zealand, South Africa and Europe all aired the report, and people were absolutely captivated by it.

Annie didn't enjoy the attention, but she was happy because it started a discussion about the intensive farming of pigs. Food writers in Ireland questioned why consumers were being denied the option to choose free-range. They saw that other countries offered free-range pork and bacon in their supermarkets. Listeners rang talk shows asking why they had no choice. Lots of them said their children and teenagers had turned vegetarian and even vegan because of their concerns over animal welfare, and they were worried that their children would be vitamin B12 deficient. Enlightened foodies questioned why 'big food' companies were pushing plant-based meat alternatives filled with additives and made from highly processed ingredients that were flown halfway around the world.

Annie thought *plant-based meat* should mean meat produced from animals free to graze and forage as nature intended. But, instead, big food businesses had hijacked the term to mean imitation meat.

The pigs were moved from the stream. Everything went smoothly, and they were all on their best behaviour as advised by Honky. When they arrived at the farm, they discovered James had opened the sides of the shed and moved the gates to make an outdoor area for the pigs to move freely. He laid down a bed of straw so it was a more natural environment for them. All the pens were left open, and they could sleep in whichever pen they fancied. They were now free to come and go as they pleased until he organised the fields around the farm. James stood watching them as the pigs charged about, sniffing and throwing the straw up in the air. It felt good to see them so happy. Mabel and Len stood and surveyed the new set-up with satisfaction.

'We have a whole new life here now,' said Mabel. 'And it's going to get even better.'

Farmer Herbert led Mikey up the lane. Mikey had had his feet professionally pared, and he felt like he was walking on air. James had prepared a small shed that had been used to store fencing material for the donkey. Outside, Mikey could see over the fence into the pigs' new free-ranging area. As James led him in, he assured Mikey that it was just temporary.

'As soon as I have the fields organised and fenced, you will be outside,' he said. 'You'll all be outside, and it will be your job to look after the pigs.'

James was looking forward to this brand-new world on his farm.

Annie drove in the gate minutes after the pigs returned with Hugo in the passenger seat. His mother had phoned her and said Hugo was bereft not seeing his pals.

'Annie, would you talk to James and see if he'd allow Hugo to visit? I've never seen him so upset. I think he'll be reassured if he can see them and see that they're okay.'

Hugo jumped out of Annie's car and ran to Mikey, burying his face into the donkey's neck and wrapping his arms around him. As Mikey nuzzled Hugo back, his top lip began curling.

'Wait for it...,' warned Honky as she lowered her head and clamped her front feet to her ears.

Mikey threw his head back and gave a loud series of joyful HEEEEEE-HAAAAAWs that echoed and reverberated around the sheds, making everyone laugh.

38.

The Partnership

Annie and James strolled around the farm, planning what needed to be done to allow the pigs more freedom. Annie made lots of suggestions as they walked around the fields, discussing the new layout excitedly.

Suddenly, James stopped and turned to her.

'Annie, how do you feel about coming into partnership with me?'

'A partnership? Do you want me to buy into your farm?'

'Well, not initially. I need your expertise more, so I can establish a new rare breed herd.'

He explained he would sell his weaners but replace them with some rare breed bloodlines.

'I will keep Len to keep the family genetics going, but he is due to retire soon anyway.'

'What about the sows and Hugo's favourite, you know, the one he calls Mabel?' she asked.

'I'll keep them all for breeding. There is no harm crossing them initially with a rare breed boar.'

James told Annie of all his plans, and she loved his imaginative and progressive proposals for the farm. She agreed to advise, and yes, maybe invest in the farm in the future.

'But one thing, James, would you allow Hugo to come down on weekends and during school holidays to help on the farm?'

She knew that Hugo caused James many sleepless nights because of his actions, and she wouldn't have been too surprised if the farmer refused.

But James was too excited about the future to hold any grudges. Besides, he was fascinated by the boy.

'Of course, he can come here. He's brilliant with animals. Have you seen how he seems to be able to communicate with them? The animals look at him and even seem to respond. It's almost as if he's talking to them. It's extraordinary to watch.'

Annie wondered how James would react to one last request.

'Honky is outgrowing the woodshed. She is never going to fit in with the rest of my pigs, and I worry about her being alone...'

She didn't have to say any more.

'Honky can come and live here with Mikey and the rest of the pigs. I could use her to keep the newly-weaned piglets company, and she would be free to come and go as she pleases.' They agreed that Honky would move to James' farm as soon as he organised his fields.

'That's fantastic!' said Annie, beaming. 'I don't think it would be possible to confine her to my place anyway. I have no idea how she is getting out and getting up here. I'm beginning to think she can open gates and doors.'

39.

Honky & Hugo

Hugo started to cry. Deep gulping and shoulder-shuddering crying. Annie was startled and immediately pulled in her car. She thought that Hugo would be happy with all the news she had to share, and now he was wailing as if his world was about to end.

Oh, good lord, what did I say? I can't bring him back to his mother like this, she thought.

'Hugo, why are you crying? I thought it would be the best news ever. Honky will be delighted. Mabel and the pigs are safe and happy, and Mikey has a lovely new home. So why are you crying?'

Hugo couldn't answer. He just bawled even louder. She handed him a box of tissues and waited for the tears to subside. Eventually, he calmed down enough to tell her.

'You're crying with relief? Oh, Hugo, you lovely, lovely boy. Come here.'

With that, she enveloped him in her arms and held him close.

'You know, it's a real gift to be able to communicate with animals and for them to understand and trust you?'

Hugo didn't answer. He was used to people teasing him for being 'odd' or making excuses for his strange behaviours. He wasn't used to praise, especially for his communications skills.

'It takes all sorts to make a world, and if everyone was the same, things would never change. Because of your actions, you forced James to rethink what he was doing. Now he has changed everything on the farm, and the lives of all the animals have improved. You have made some great friends, and thanks to you, one donkey's life has been transformed, and there are lots of very happy and relieved pigs on James' farm.'

She beamed at Hugo.

'Now dry your eyes, and come home with me and tell Honky the good news.'

Hugo jumped out of the car when they arrived at Annie's farm, and he ran off to find Honky. The pair sat under the yew tree, and he told her everything. Honky didn't say a word for a while.

'The problem is I will miss Annie if I'm living there,' she said. 'And if I stay here, I will miss Mikey, Mabel and the others.'

Hugo assured her that Annie was likely to spend as much time on James' farm as her own farm. He explained how James had asked her to help, advise and invest in his new pig farm.

'But I have so much freedom here. Will I have as much there, do you think?'

'Of course you will!' said Hugo. 'Annie and I will make sure of that, and James says that you will become the 'face' of the new Boarswood Pig Farm. You'll be on all his packaging and be expected to meet and greet all the people who come to his new farm shop.'

'That's so exciting!' Honky said, and she did several of her happy spins, making Hugo laugh out loud for the first time in ages.

'I did a bit of reading about Boarswood the other night,' he said. 'Did you know it got its name originally because it was a deep, dense wooded area where wild boar roamed long before human settlers arrived?'

'That means that Mabel's stories were all true,' Honky said. 'She always said it was an ancestral memory.'

Hugo had other news to share with Honky. His mother and father finally listened when he told them how unhappy he was at school.

'They went to the school in the next village and spoke to the headmaster there. They have lots of autistic children in the school and have extra teachers to help them. I'm going to spend my last year in primary there.'

Hugo glowed with happiness at the prospect of never returning to his old school again.

Hugo's father had also suggested that he work hard so that he could have a career in engineering. He gave him a book written by an American scientist called Temple Grandin, an animal behavioural expert who is autistic. She designed calming systems for animals in abattoirs to minimise stress.

'Animals hate loud banging noises, terrible smells and bright lights,' Hugo's father told him. 'Because she's autistic, she understands how stressful that is.'

'She's like me, and animals are like me. There are lots of others like me,' Hugo said, relieved to discover he wasn't alone. 'There are lots of 'different' types of folk and animals in this world.'

Honky snuggled up to him, rubbed her snout into the boy's jumper and sighed with content.

'I'm so glad you're the way you are, Hugo,' she said, 'and I hope you never change!'

Acknowledgements

To my children, Patrick and Sadb Shaffrey, for putting up with my pig obsession.

Thanks to Mary Gilvarry Rogan for your endless support and encouragement to keep going.

Thanks too to Susan Duffy for understanding how much Honky meant to me and rolling up your sleeves so many times to help.

Grateful appreciation to Grainne Flynn and John and Madison Hatton for keeping my spirits up by constantly keeping in touch.

To my 'pigwimmin' pals: Martha Roberts, Helen Joy and Susan Tanner - always willing to give advice and support.

And thanks to my neighbours Denis Sutton and Larry Murphy for dropping what you were doing to give me a dig out!

Also special thanks to Carole Byrne, physiotherapist by appointment to 'HRH'.

About the Author

Margaret studied Agriculture and Food Science and later spent many years working in the food industry in quality management. When she was made redundant in 2009, she went down the path of growing her own food and rearing pigs and poultry. Honky was born on her small-holding and although the publication is a work of fiction, a large percentage of the story is true. She relocated from north Meath (where the story is based) to south Wexford 2018 where Honky sadly died.

Please Review

Dear reader, If you enjoyed this book, I would really appreciate if you could leave a review on Amazon or Goodreads. Your opinion counts and it does influence buyer decisions on whether to purchase the book or not. Reviews can also open doors to new and bigger audiences for the author and helps get this book into the hands of those who most need to hear its message

Lightning Source UK Ltd.
Milton Keynes UK
UKHW020052301121
394795UK00006B/781